THE LIGHTHOUSE

Professor Joseph Henry
First Secretary of the Smithsonian Institute and Chairman of the Lighthouse Board. Cabinet photograph by Henry Ulke, 1875. Courtesy of the Smithsonian Institution Archives.

THE LIGHTHOUSE

THAT

WANTED TO STAY LIT

ERNEST HENRY WAKEFIELD
with contributions from
GEORGE PATTERSON WAKEFIELD - THEODORE DUNMORE WAKEFIELD
KAREN CORNELIUS - RANDY K. STRAUSS

Ernest H. Wakefield
Honors Press Inc.
2300 Noyes Ct., Suite 511
Evanston IL 60201

International Standard Book Number: 0-943465-54-0
Ernest H. Wakefield of Evanston IL 60201

Dedicated

to

Commodore Frederick William Wakefield

and his wife

Mary Poley Wakefield

Together they built *Harbor View* which forms the genesis of

the Inland Seas Maritime Museum

TABLE OF CONTENTS

ILLUSTRATIONS

FOREWORD

How lucky for us that the trustees of the Great Lakes Historical Society approved, on the 200th anniversary of the U. S. Lighthouse Service, a project to rebuild the handsome 1877-1929 Vermilion, Ohio lighthouse. Appropriately it stands today on the lakefront of the Inland Seas Maritime Museum in Vermilion

Many facts about the lighthouse have been printed in diverse media. We are now doubly lucky because all the known history of the lighthouse has been brought together in a book, *The Lighthouse That Wanted To Stay Lit.*

Built on the west pierhead during the Golden Age of wood shipbuilding in Vermilion's small harbor, it served as its beacon and symbol for sixty–two years, long enough for those persons sixty-five years or older to remember it fondly still. One of these persons is younger brother Ernest H. Wakefield, author and compiler of the only bound collection of facts on the lighthouse. He was only fifteen years of age when the beacon was disassembled and barged away to oblivion (careful research has never revealed its fate). Although I am two years older than he, his memory is sometimes better than mine. That's why I have to label some of its contents *historical fiction.*

Humans develop a sense of place by connecting with other humans who shared a particular corner of the earth and called it home. The fund raising for the replica lighthouse was dubbed "Vermilion's 1877 Lighthouse Project." The monetary and gifts-in-kind response was heavy from Vermilion. However, generous donations came from visiting yachtsmen, sons of former lighthouse keepers, grandsons of lighthouse builders, former Vermilion residents, summer visitors, and just plain old lighthouse buffs who have nostalgic feelings toward these unique structures.

We can only conclude: *Everyone loves a lighthouse!.*

January 15, 1992

Theodore D. Wakefield

19 Simara Street

Sewall's Point, Florida 34996

PREFACE

The 1877 Vermilion lighthouse is one of my earliest memories. Until 1929 the structure was a sentinel on the west pier of the Vermilion harbor. As a boy I, with others, would play tag around the lighthouse unconcerned that below its narrow ledges lay hard, jagged, and mossy sandstone rocks emerging from the swishing lake water. In these half-hidden interstices I would also fish for rock bass.

Beyond the harbor there were sailboats races. I was yet too young to participate, but with a few gymnastics I was able to perch on the elevated, narrow, eight-inch fender facing the lake and lean against the back-slanting body of the lighthouse. From this vantage point I could view the competition unimpeded by the heads of spectators taller than I. While I was never invited within the lantern to view the Fresnel lens, in later life I have visited similar lofty lanterns in other lighthouses. There, I witnessed the glory of the physicist's science and the magnificence of the glasscutter's and glasscaster's art, activities now rare.

As I became older and was selected to record the vessel's name and time of arrival in long distance sailing races, typically near midnight, I would sit on the hard and oftentimes cold rocks near this lighthouse engrossed in being the scribe.

Until 1923, extending some 500 feet upriver from the lighthouse, there was a steel skeleton walkway elevated above the western rock pier. On this structure a wooden and concrete walkway permitted the lighthouse keeper to twice daily reach the lighthouse dry shod even with the lake rolling heavily and with the pier awash. On the automation of the light, this serviceable bridge- structure was disassembled and removed by the U. S. Lighthouse Service. Some of the nuts, twice too heavy, I purloined and used for sinkers on my fishing gill nets. And some of the long, thick, tread-wood forms we boys used as ugly, model boats along the nearby sand beach. Interestingly this beach immediately west of the lighthouse pier is exactly the same now as it was seventy years earlier. Instead of my brothers and I using it as a playground with our friends, it is now a like area for my grand nieces and grand nephews. The two stone piers, however, still discipline the stream as it flows placidly to the lake, just as in former times. What is different is the greater number of pleasure craft that crease its surface.

The privilege of maturing in this excellent environment for children I owe to my father. As a boy of ten he worked a ten-hour day in England turning a large flywheel driving a printing press. He arrived in America at thirteen with his family, attending school, working in Cleveland steel mills, clerking in a shop specializing in fine bric-a-brac. He would eventually own his own manufacturing company. Becoming a yachtsman, as his affluence increased, he learned of the Vermilion 1877 lighthouse and the wonderful harbor it guarded. Impressed with the environment for raising his growing family he moved his company to the town.

Remembering his own austere early years he would, before bedtime, tell his children, "*You* can wake up in the morning and *play* all day," a pleasure he seldom knew as a boy.

That promise we did with a vengeance: boat building, sailing, swimming, skating, ice-boating, sledding, etc., but only after completing the many chores too often absent from the life of boys and girls today.

In organization this book has: 1) a rather extensive Front Section, 2) a Text of three chapters which relates the story of both the 1877 Vermilion Lighthouse and its Replica, 3) a Back Section composed of: 4) a section on Additional Readings, 5) a series of eight Appendices which more fully presents the lighthouse environment, 6) a Glossary, and 7) an Index.

It is with utmost pleasure that I write this memento concerning the Vermilion Lighthouse. The writings about the structure by Karen Cornelius, Editor of the *Vermilion Photojournal,* have been most helpfull as has the photography of Wallis Wheatley, and others who are cited. In addition, Karen has provided the interesting reporting which appears as Appendix D. The photograph of Professor Joseph Henry in the Frontispiece was kindly furnished by Dr. Marc Rothenberg and Kathleen W. Dorman of the Joseph Henry Papers Collection of the Smithsonian Institution. The text by Randy K. Strauss, President, Strauss Construction Inc., and drawings by Robert Lee Tracht, architect, were helpful. The list of donors in Appendix H was provided by Martha Long from the staff of the Inland Seas Maritime Museum.

Additional aid in writing this book have been my yet surviving brothers: George Patterson Wakefield, and Theodore "Ted" Dunmore Wakefield both of whom have spent their entire lives in Vermilion. They and their wives, Mary and Margaret, have read the entire text. All four have been intensely interested in maritime affairs so may be considered experts on activities associated with Vermilion. Errors, if any, are my own. Where Ted, in his historical search about the 1877 Vermilion lighthouse, ran into blanks, I have completed the file with what I believe to be reasonable assumptions romantically attuned.

Captain R. A. Schultz, Chief, Aids to Navigation and Waterways Management Branch, and Planning Officer W. H. Craig of Ninth Coast Guard District both kindly forwarded information clarifying the concept of *order* as applied to Fresnel lenses.

Almost surely this book was able to be published in time, 6 June 1992, for the dedication of the Replica 1877 Vermilion Lighthouse only because of the generosity of the trustees of the Great Lakes Historical Society.

In reproducing this manuscript the services of Mildred L. Wiesser, Robert T. Schreiber of the Center for Manufacturing Engineering, and Frances Glass-Newmann of the Program of Master of Management in Manufacturing, all of Northwestern University, Evanston, Illinois, have been most helpful. Finally, I wish to thank Apple Computer Inc. for aid in computer services.

Ernest Henry Wakefield

Evanston, Illinois

INTRODUCTION

A lighthouse as a beacon for ships bound for a port is almost as old as is civilization. The world's first lighthouse, Pharos, one of the seven wonders of the ancient world, stood on an island before the Rosetta estuary of the Nile river. Pharos, as a navigational aid for ships plying the eastern Mediterranean Sea, bore a wood fire at all times to identify from the sea the city of Alexandria, the principle port of Egypt. Pharos was built by Ptolemy II in 280 B. C. and was destroyed by an earthquake in the 14th century.

Pharos is believed to have been constructed of limestone to a height of some one-hundred feet. Combustibles for the flame were borne by slaves circling ever upward on steps about its perimeter. Pharos marked the port to which the fleets of Cleopatra and Mark Anthony fled after their defeat by the galleys of Augustus Caesar in 31 B. C. at the sea battle of Actium, off the northwest coast of what is today Greece.

In the development of the lighthouse from the

above ancient times to the present, two requirements have been sought: 1) A suitable light source, and 2) a means of directing the light to a vessel at sea. These two developments are discussed below.

THE DEVELOPMENT OF LIGHT SOURCES

Essential to a lighthouse, therefore, is a light source. Better it be small and intense. These two requirements would not be easily satisfied until the latter half of the 19th century and then only in a few lighthouses. A second ingredient for a modern lighthouse is its lens system. Pharos had none. The night vision of land from the sea is an indigo enigma. How to mark rock-outcroppings, islands, and harbors in sea lanes? Therefore, to identify these nautical elements lighthouses were built early in human communication.

Limiting the distance such a site could be seen, all other conditions being equal, was the light output of the luminous source. A candle flame can be seen by ordinary eyes at a distance of some two miles against a black background. Such sighting can be improved if a mirror-reflector directs the light-rays toward the ship. Until the middle of the 19th century an oil-burning flame was used as a light source where the combustible was olive oil or whale-oil. The latter burns more cleanly.

In 1800 Alessandro Volta of Pavia, building on the earlier work of Luigi Galvani, a professor of anatomy at Bologna, announced if a disc of copper and a disc of zinc were separated by a blotter saturated with salt water a continuous flow of electricity could be withdrawn. Volta called this assembly a *pile.* And today the Italian word for the English word *battery* is *pila.* Volta's invention of the battery is recognized as one of the greatest scientific discoveries of all time. Where before one could obtained only *bursts* of electricity from rubbing a glass rod with fur of an animal,[1] for example, now for the first time a continuous flow of electricity was available from an electrical battery.

---

1. *Frictional electricity:* when two dissimilar substances are rubbed together, they become oppositely electrified; and if either is an insulator, it retains a charge. This process is known technically as *triboelectrification.*

Because England was at war with France Volta wrote two identical letters to Sir Joseph Banks, President of the London Royal Society, hoping one would penetrate the blockade. Banks, a botanist, had earlier completed a round-the-world voyage with Captain James Cook, on a ship of which the Sailing Master was Lieutenant William Bligh. He was known later as Captain Bligh for *The Mutiny on the Bounty.* [2] Within ten days of Volta's message reaching Banks, William Nicholson and Anthony Carlisle observed water could be separated into hydrogen and oxygen by the passage of electricity through the fluid. The science of electrochemistry had been born!

---

2. Captain William Bligh was seriously maligned by the authors of *Mutiny on the Bounty*. While authoritarian he was an able officer. Originally sent to Tahiti to transfer breadfruit trees to the Caribbean as a food for slaves on British sugar-producing islands, he not only returned to Tahiti, captured a number of mutineers, but transported them to England where several were hanged. In addition, Bligh did succeed in transplanting breadfruit to the Caribbean. Ironically, the slaves preferred the native plantain, a specie of tropical fruit which resembles a banana, but is longer, more green, less sweet and contains more starch. Subsequently Bligh became a respected admiral in the British Navy. Plantains are seen in American city markets.

Continuing experimentation with Volta's batteries in 1801, Sir Humphrey Davy, placing many of Volta's cells in series, was able to generate sufficient voltage to create the first incandescent carbon-arc light source. Such a source may have offered a thousand-fold luminous intensity increase over an oil-wick flame, for in a lighthouse the intensity of the source is all important.

By this experiment electricity, it was learned, could create light! Almost immediately carbon- arcs were considered as a light source for lighthouses. But batteries, the source of energy, have a limited life. Lighthouses, however, during night and while fog is extent need a continuous light source. A solution was on its way.

In 1821 Michael Faraday found that an electric current flowing in a wire, if suitably placed near a magnet, produced rotary motion. It was not until 1832, however, would Hippolyte Pixii demonstrate an operating electric motor before the *Acadamie des Sciences* in Paris. A battery was its energy source. And in 1861 Antonio Pacinotti realized that a proper ring-assembly of iron, copper wire and insulation was a motor if a battery were applied to the pair of wires, *and* a generator of electricity if mechanical power were applied to the assembly instead. Thus a motor and a generator, he proclaimed, may be one and the same object. Now all motor/generators are of the ring assembly type devised by Pacinotti. In 1869 Zénobe Théophile Gramme confirmed Pacinotti's observations and created the first motor/ generator capable of generating one horsepower. Gramme soon employed a steam engine to supply mechanical power to the generator. Now there could be a steady flow of electric power in great quantity. Carbon-arc lamps could then be considered for lighthouses.

Charles K. Hyde points out there was designed in 1853 an effective light source for lighthouses with from one to four concentric wicks.[3] The light output depending on the

---

3. Charles K. Hyde. *The Northern Lights: Lighthouses of the Upper Great Lakes.* Volume VI of the Michigan Heritage Series, Michigan Natural Resources Magazine, Box 30034 Lansing, Michigan 48909.

number. This light source was developed by General George C. Meade. It was Meade who was to repel Robert E. Lee's Confederate assaults at Gettysburg in 1863.

Because of the decrease in sperm whale harvest oil for light sources increased from 50 cents per gallon in 1840 to $2.25 per gallon in 1855 forcing the Lighthouse Board to seek a cheaper alternative. The alternative found by Professor Joseph Henry of the Smithsonian Institute was the use of lard oil, a source which illuminated well if preheated. As the result of these tests lard oil became the common energy source, the Lighthouse Service consuming 100,000 gallons of lard oil annually.

On 27 August 1859 oil was discovered in Pennsylvania by Edwin Laurentine Drake. In the same year the kerosene-burning lantern was developed. This very versatile light source, burning a cheap and plentiful fuel, gradually replaced whale-oil lamps in lighthouses. The ensuing American Civil War, 1861-1865, caused the American whaling fleet precipitously to decline, never to recover. The fortunate discovery of petroleum, together with numerous other factors, also probably saved whales from extinction. Several types of light sources were now available for lighthouses. Lighthouse directors could employ carbon-arcs as a source of light, a light far more luminous than an oil lamp or kerosene source. In 1862 a carbon-arc light was installed in a lighthouse on the south coast of Kent, England. A carbon-arc was also installed in a lighthouse in Havre, France in 1863, using a direct-current generator assembled by Pixii. About this time Paul Jablochkoff placed a hollow, translucent kaolin cylinder around a carbon-arc, causing it to yield a more pleasing light which, while less applicable for lighthouses, could light a hall.

While a reflecting mirror could be and was used in a lighthouse with a carbon-arc light source, just as with an oil lamp, Augustin Jean Fresnel introduced a better system. A French physicist Fresnel in the early 19th century conceived stacking a series of circular prisms of varying diameter to form a hollow sphere around the light source. Such an assembly can be designed to direct a beam of light in a plane parallel to the water surface, and thus to vessels at sea. Tests by the British Bureau of Lighthouse Service found the Fresnel system to be some five-times more visible at sea than the reflecting mirror for the same light source.

While carbon-arcs are indeed luminous, they need constant adjustment as the carbon burns away. In addition, they emit a smoke of tiny carbon particles, causing the highly polished lens invented by Fresnel to become gradually more opaque. This coating dulled the advantage of Fresnel's optics.

All the above information was soon known by the U. S. Lighthouse Service then headed by Professor Joseph Henry, a physicist also serving as Director of the Smithsonian Institution. Many lighthouses in the United States, bearing oil-wick lamps, were successively equipped with Fresnel lens nearly all of which were made in France.

In 1879 Thomas Edison in the United States and Sir Joseph Wilson Swan in England invented the incandescent lamp wherein electricity, in passing through a conducting filament, heats it to incandescence in an evacuated enclosure.

Such an assembly yields a safe, totally enclosed light source of great intensity. Constantly improved, the incandescent lamp eventually replaced carbon- arcs in even the most powerful lighthouses, and oil lamps and kerosene lanterns in smaller lighthouses.

Meanwhile, toward the end of the century, with the refining of petroleum into lighter and more volatile liquids, gasoline became plentiful. This availability led to the development of the high pressure gasoline lamp. In this light source fine gasoline mist is emitted through an orifice enclosed in a small cloth bag, the fibers of which have been impregnated with the rare earths thoria and ceria. When the mist is ignited the cloth bag is consumed, but the mantle remains, yielding a most intense white light. Such a light source was devised by the Austrian chemist Carl Auer von Welsbach. This light source was used in a few lighthouses. Such gasoline pressure lamps bearing Welsbach mantles are used today in sporting forays into the field. The mantle, being only ash, is, however, most friable.

With the advent of the automobile, acetylene, a highly inflammable colorless gas easily generated, could serve as a light source for lighthouses. Such an intense light source soon replaced the wick oil lamp in many lighthouses.

The carbon arc-lamp is the antecedent of the gaseous-discharge lamp now commonly seen as fluorescent lamps. These light sources, being large and of low brightness, are particularly used for room and space lighting. The first American commercial fluorescent installation was designed and sold by the author in August 1937 and installed in McGarvey's restaurant in Vermilion.

Where intense beams are required, as in a lighthouse, a further descendant of the gaseous-discharge lamp is the mercury-halogen, high-pressure lamps commonly seen in late-model automobile headlamps and on some city streets.

The light source employed in the Inland Seas Marine Museum lighthouse employs a coil-coiled filament, incandescent lamp with clear glass, filled with argon gas, a light source developed in the late 1930s. To obtain a red-colored beam a hollow cylinder of transparent red glass encloses the incandescent lamp. To automatically control the on-off cycle of the lamp, a solar cell, sensing the degree of darkness, controls an electric switch. While the 1877 Vermilion lighthouse employed a lighthouse-keeper from 1877 to about 1922 when solar cell controls were introduced, no like-person is required for the Inland Seas Maritime Museum. The light is automatic.

Just as the story of light sources, sketched above, has interest, no less arresting is the development of lenses for lighthouses.

THE FRESNEL LENS

The person who most influenced lighthouse design worldwide was almost surely Augustin Jean Fresnel, (1788-1827) . Fresnel was born at Broglie, near Caen in French Normandy to middle-class parents. After attending the well-regulated Caen school, his parents sent him to the *École Polytechnique*, then to the *École des Ponts et Chaussées*. Thereafter, he was employed by the royal state in designing and building of bridges and roads.

While lenses for light had been known since the year 1039, Galileo Galilei (1564-1642) had used a lens equipped telescope in discovering several of the moons of Jupiter. Little, however, was known of the nature of light. In his free time Fresnel pursued optics, a science dominated by Sir Isaac Newton (1642-1727) and his corpuscular theory of light. Newton, one of the greatest scientist who ever lived, had such prestige that his theory of light was everywhere believed for nearly one-hundred and fifty years.

With Napoleon's triumphal return from the island of Elba after his first banishment Fresnel, a supporter of Louis XVIII, opposed him. Later he lost his state position under the Empire. In this enforced freedom Fresnel carried on experiments in optics, particularly on the diffraction of light. His intense work in optics began in 1815, after the Battle of Waterloo. With the resulting restoration of royalty, he again was given his state position. Independently he came to the conclusion that light was propagated as a wave form. His friend, Dominique François Arago, called his attention to the papers of Dr. Thomas Young, the English physicist and physician, with whom Fresnel was unacquainted because of the Napoleonic wars' blockade.

Young, with his experiments, also was pursuaded to the wave theory. He had, indeed, been so severely attacked by fellow scientists for his beliefs he abandonned the study of optics and afterwards devoted himself to hieroglyphic research. In this task he succeeded in deciphering the Rosetta Stone found in Egypt by an officer from Napoleon's forces near the original site of Pharos.

Fresnel brought to his research "an ingenious mind, deft hands, and the discipline of an excellent scientific education" and succeeded in winning an ever increasing number of scientists to the wave theory of light. Towards the end of his life Fresnel devoted his considerable knowledge in optics to the French Bureau of Lighthouses. His optic designs for lighthouses affected the entire world. He died of tuberculosis in his home in Broglie 14 July 1827. His extraordinary creative life was nine years.

The *Encyclopedia Americana* describes some 27 categories of lenses. A most remarkable example of a Fresnel lens, of *order 2*, disassembled from the Spectacle Reef lighthouse in northern Lake Huron, is in the Inland Seas Maritime Museum. A simpler one also graces and directs the light of the Replica 1877 Vermilion Lighthouse.

THE LIGHTHOUSE THAT WANTED TO STAY LIT

Chapter 1
HISTORY OF THE VERMILION RIVER BUILDING & TRANSPORTING THE 1877 VERMILION LIGHTHOUSE

Geologically speaking the Vermilion river is a relatively recent stream dating to only the most recent ice-age, the *Wisconsin Advance*, of the *Pleistocene Epoch* some ten-thousand years ago. A talisman is the sharp, lofty shale banks some two miles upriver. In deposits of this period skeletons of early mankind and of mankind-like animals have been found.

The first riffles on the river's placid surface could have been made by fish schooling along its weedy banks. Wandering muskrats migrating from an older stream might next have disturbed its waters. Then some few thousand year ago Indians exploring for an overnight campsite as a respite from the boisterous lake could have broken the surface with their paddles. Later migrants going upsteam discovered the ochre clays which gave the name of Vermilion to

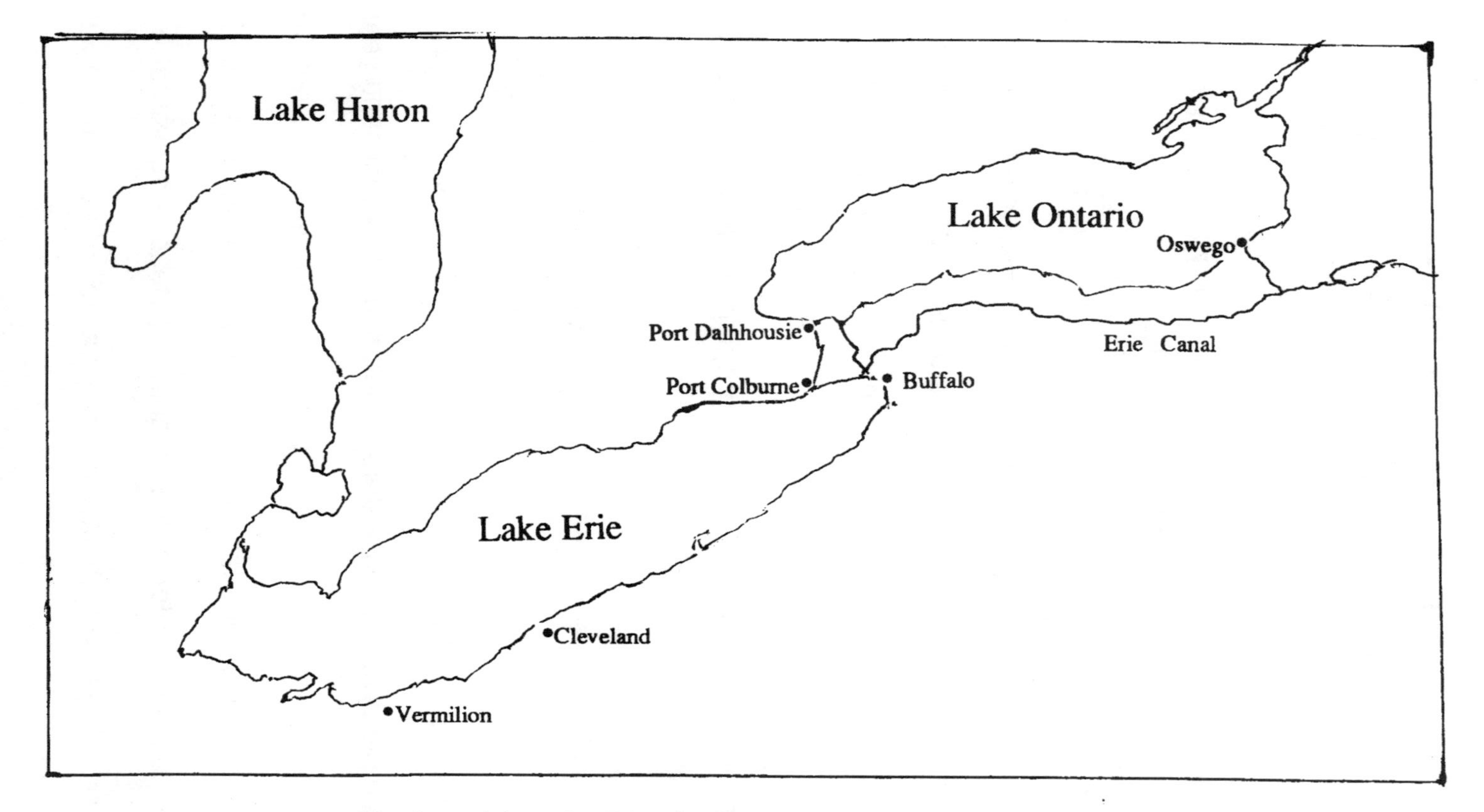

The lower lakes, the Erie, and Welland Canals. Ernest H. Wakefield

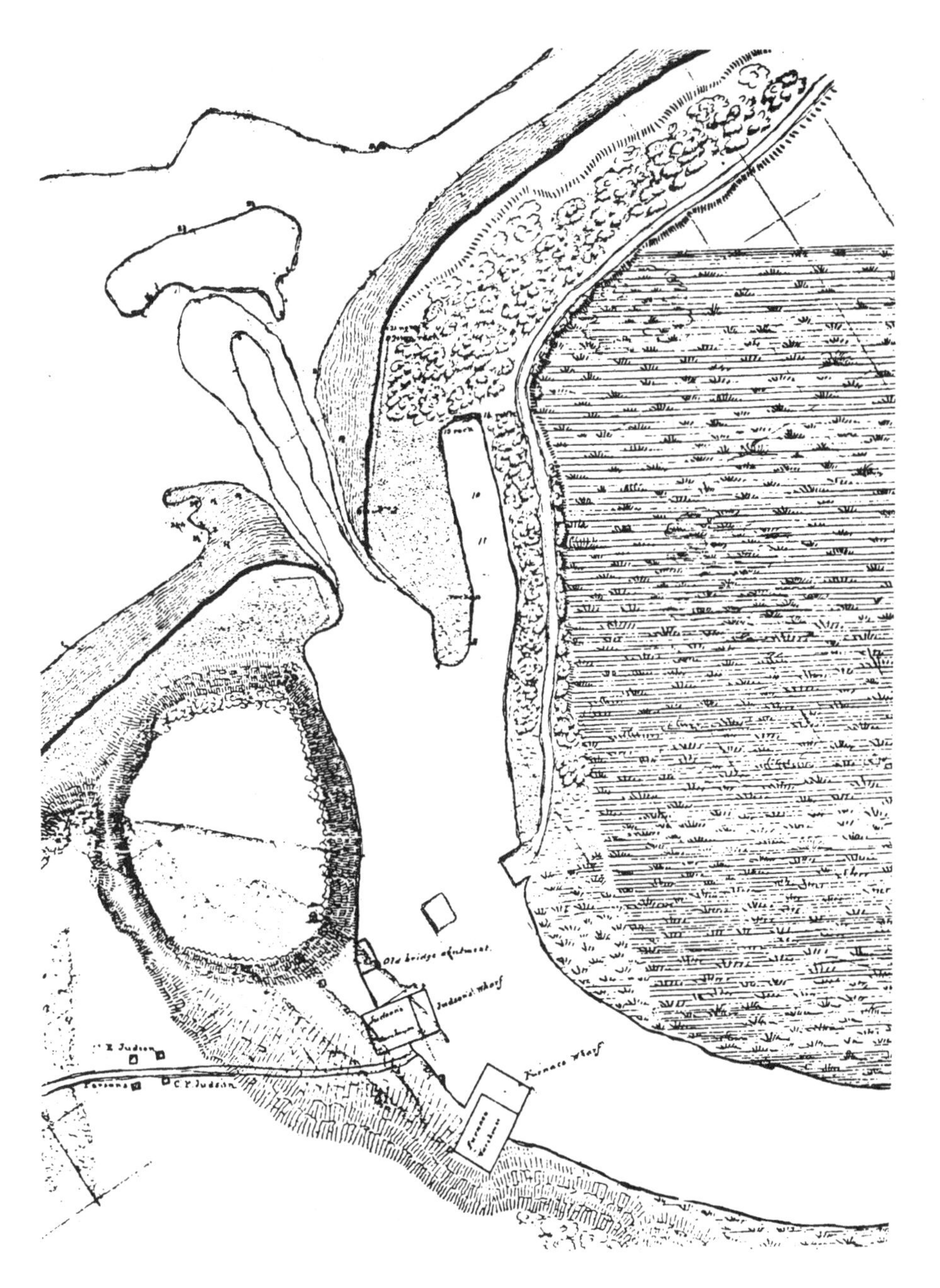

An 1833 chart of the lower section of Vermilion river. George P. Wakefield

the river. The Erie Indians, almost exterminated by the Iroquois in 1656 whose hunting grounds bordered the area, gave the name to this large body of water.

Lake Erie, being most southern of the Great Lakes, was missed by the exploring and ambitious French. *Voyageurs* passed, with their provision laden *batteaux,* from the more northern lying Saint Lawrence river, up the Ottawa river, then the Mattawa river, Lake Nipissing, French river, continuing across Georgian Bay, through the North Channel, up the St. Mary's river and finally into the great waters of Lake Superior. Animal furs were their quarry; the Indians their ally. This voyage, made during the French period, is alluded to in Appendix A as is a 1656 map of Lake Erie. The last Vermilion Indian, Fred Platte, well known to the author, is characterized in Appendix B.

Theodore Dunmore Wakefield of Vermilion, Ohio, cognizant of this French exploration, in 1987 offered a one-thousand dollar prize for the name of the discoverer of Lake Erie. Seized upon by historians the reward encouraged Conrad Heidenreich to discover a trace of the lake on animal skin dated 1641. This relic has been displayed in the Huronic Museum at Midland, Ontario. Its unveiling by the Governor-General of Canada and its presentation to the public was a recent historical high point.

The American westward movement continued, two hundred miles a generation. Ohio became a state on 1 March 1803. With the waning of Indian influence, the lake fish population being so plentiful, fishermen soon settled on the banks of what became known as the Vermilion river. First they used along-shore seines. Then, venturing farther onto the lake, they would set pound and gill-nets from large flat-bottom, easily built rowboats.

In the spring of the year, water from the many

emerging farms surrounding the river would cascade into rivulets, form into runs, combine into creeks, swell into branches, and finally flood into the Vermilion river causing a freshet. At such time pig-styes, fence posts, and even chickens living in the valley of the river might be swept into the maelstrom. The current carried them rapidly downstream into the lake, the flotsam and jetsam being deposited on the nearby beaches.

After the flood had subsided, the waves and long-shore-currents in the lake would carry sand from the beaches and largely close the little river. As a result sailing and oared fish boats could no longer easily reach their docks to unload the catches. A period map of the Vermilion river is enclosed. In 1838 the citizens of the small town of Vermilion, led by the fishermen, erected wooden stakes at the harbor entrance. On these supports they secured an oil-burning beacon.

To maintain the navigable harbor after the freshet

the fishermen petitioned their congressman and through him to secure a congressional appropriation. These funds would allow the U. S. Corps of Engineers to dredge the river and build two piers to both constrict the river and prevent the along-shore currents from filling the freshet-opened channel. A chart of the river and nearby soundings is also enclosed.

The operation completed Vermilion now had a government-maintained harbor. Please see Appendix F. With this tranformation in 1847, fourteen years before the American War Between the States, the U. S. Lighthouse Board placed a more permanent beacon at the porthead. In his researches with the U. S. National Archives Theodore D. Wakefield writes:

"According to William F. Sherman from the Archives, the Vermilion Lighthouse ...'was built on a pier in 1847, rebuilt in 1859 and again in 1877.' Letters from the Tenth Light House District to the Light House Board show that the tower and lantern were shipped from Buffalo to Oswego and transported to Vermilion in the Tender *Haze*, assigned to the jurisdiction of the

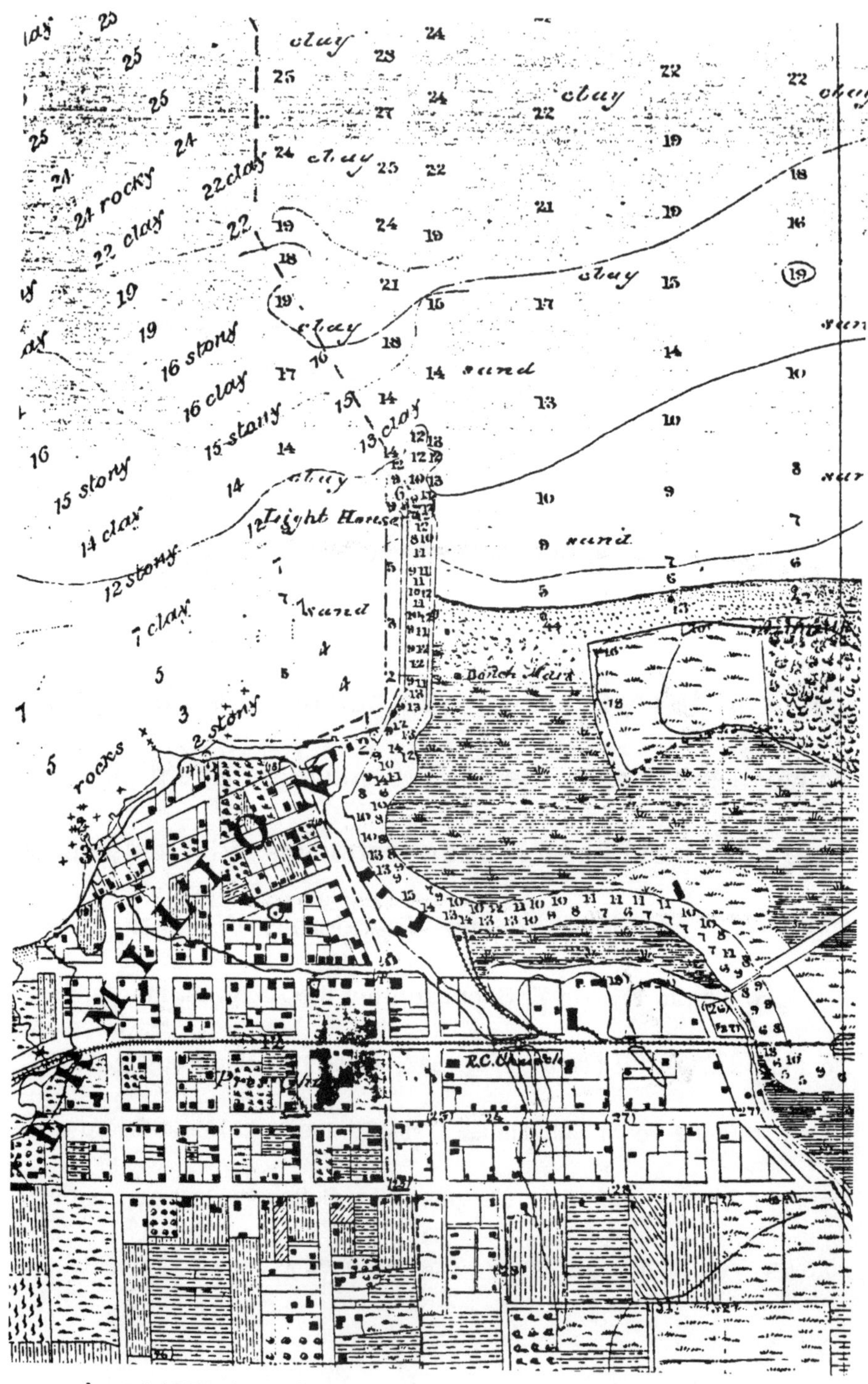

A post 1877 chart of the Vermilion river. Theodore D. Wakefield

A Vermilion schooner of the 19th century. Ernest H. Wakefield

District Inspector. The Engineer suggested using the lens formerly used at Erie Harbor for the Vermilion lighthouse, or ordering a new one, but I found no indication of which was done. The sixth order lens used in 1859 was replaced by the fifth order Fresnel lens made by the Paris firm of Barbier and Fenestre[1], but I have not been able to find out whether it was ordered in the1870's or was already on hand at the Light House Depot in Norfolk.

"'I have also found from the records that the lighthouse was moved in 1893 closer to the end of the pier, and that in 1919 the oil lamp was replaced by an acetylene lamp in stock at Buffalo. I did not find out from the records what was done with the oil lamp at the time the change was made. The Vermilion light was put under the care of the assistant keeper at Lorain, and in the early 1920's the house that had been used as the keeper's residence in Vermilion was sold to the Masonic Lodge in that city.'"

As the result of this harbor improvement, facilities were eventually constructed for building schooners, transporting fuel, wheat, and supplies. The reader should view the map showing this improvement. A major activity near the mouth of the river was the unloading of schooners bearing limestone.

---

1. The concept of *order* of the Fresnel lens as used above is defined in the Glossary.

Steam-powered freighters replaced schooners in bringing lumber into Vermilion. George P. Wakefield.

Cleveland, capable of serving the increasing size of vessels, gained in ascendancy. Commercial activity along the Vermilion river waned. Only fishing continued unabated, there being some dozen steam tugs and several sailing vessels.

Among the early catches were sturgeon, a primitive type of fish with scales underlaid with bone and an outer layer of shining enamel. George Patterson Wakefield tells of the capture of such a denizen in Appendix C. The flesh of the fish is known for its wonderful flavor, and its roe is considered fit for an epicurean's banquet. Perch, pike, white bass, grey bass, eelpout, whitefish, herring, carp, and catfish were also caught. Iced, the fish were boxed and shipped to cities by way of the New York Central railroad, now Conrail.

In the marsh, on the east side of the river rabbits, muskrat, mink, and earlier, beaver could be taken for fur in the fall, winter, and spring season. And in the fields and woods:

grouse, squirrel, and earlier, deer could be shot providing variety to the mess of early residents.

Traps used for fishing were pound nets, employing stakes set in the lake bottom, gill nets, and trap nets. The hauls were heavy. As late as 1929 Professor John T. Van Oosten, a piscologist from the University of Michigan, told the author Lake Erie, because of shallowness, its range of temperature, and its plankton content, was the greatest producer of fish in tonnage for any equal area in the world. In the same year Van Oosten discovered smelt in Lake Erie, a heretofore salt water fish. He said they had come through the Welland Canal. Now the smelt is common in all five Great Lakes.

In the last decades of the 20th century commercial fishing was outlawed in states bordering the Lake Erie. Recently Anna Laura Heinig Richie, who lived with her physician father and mother in Vermilion during her youth, while visiting a remote lake in Alaska, learned that fishing *aficionados* consider sport fishing off Vermilion as one of the best areas in the world. Individual walleyed pike averaging 8-10 pounds are the usual catch.

Early on at the end of the western pier a wooden structure had been erected on which an oil lamp was secured. Around the flame a red glass enclosure was placed, presenting a red light visible from the lake. A lighthouse keeper, living in the village would, each evening, light the lamp. In the morning he would quench it, fill its base with whale oil ready for relighting at day's end.

Fishermen, approaching the harbor at night, would steer their boats to the red light, and thus find the harbor. They could then unload their fish in the shanties.

Years passed and the wooden lighthouse, exposed to sun, heavy seas, and wind rotted away.

BUILDING THE 1877 VERMILION LIGHTHOUSE

As the river and pier were now under the jurisdiction of the U. S. Government, a new group from the U. S. Corps of Engineers noted the dilapidated condition of the lighthouse. In 1866 the Congress appropriated money to place an iron lighthouse on the west pier end of the Vermilion river.

A government architect designed the lighthouse.

A contract for building this more permanent beacon was let to a iron-casting company in Buffalo, New York, a city astride the western terminus of the Erie Canal. Using sand molds, three tapering rings, octahedral in shape, were cast. The iron used for melting was from unpurchased Columbian smooth-bore cannons now made obsolete from lessons learned in the 1864-65 Civil War bombardment of Fort Sumter in Charleston harbor. Union *rifled-cannon* had proved so superior to smooth-bores firing from earlier captured Fort Morgan, south of the harbor. While reduced to a pile of rubble the 1861 Confederate -captured Sumter held out until Charleston itself fell in 1865. The iron, therefore, of the 1877 Vermilion lighthouse echoed and resonated with the terrible trauma of the War Between the States. An example of a smooth-bore cannon is mounted in Vermilion's Exchange Park, and is aimed at condominiums blocking the view of the current Vermilion lighthouse.

The lighthouse base was formed by placing one ring on top of another. Then the workmen cast the upper pediment supporting the lantern section. Finally the builders constructed the lantern section. It is unclear from the communication above from where the Fresnel lens came, the Light House Depot in Norfolk or from the French firm. The 1877 Vermilion lighthouse from the beginning was equipped with lens of the finest quality. With the iron work finished the parts of the beacon were fitted and erected to determine if all parts conveniently joined. All the workmen shouted hosannas to see the results of their noble work.

Later a small garage-sized oil-structure for the lighthouse was built.

TRANSPORTING THE 1877 VERMILION LIGHTHOUSE

The workmen disassembled the lighthouse and placed the parts on two barges lying in the nearby Erie Canal. Oil for the lighthouse would originally be kept in the keeper's residence. In the meantime, the Fresnel lens was shipped to Cleveland by train. The barges were loaded, shipping papers in order, a mule was hitched to each barge. Thus began the long voyage of the 1877 Vermilion Lighthouse. Why east through the canal, as shown in the Figure, and on to Oswego, New York rather than loading the lighthouse directly on board a lighthouse tender at the port of Buffalo is unknown.

As the mules followed the towpath the series of barges

bearing the lighthouse moved in the canal through green farm country frocked with trees and past small towns. Everywhere the local people looked at the strange load gliding by, for how many had seen the makings of a lighthouse? Every five miles a new mule replaced the former. At night each barge crew moored their vessel to the bank; the released mules were led to a manger. The men and mules then supped, slept, the former in a small cabin before the transom of the barge, readying for the next work day.

Each day the barge would be locked through the canal passing from one level of water to another. Within two week the barge-carrying lighthouse had reached Oswego, where a branch of the canal joined Lake Ontario. The Office the Lighthouse Engineer, Tenth District, realizing the summer was fast passing, urged all possible speed so the lighthouse could be installed in Vermilion while the weather was compliant.

There, in Oswego harbor, all parts of the lighthouse and the oil-house were transferred to another ship and a letter written:

Professor Joseph Henry, L. L. D.

Chairman, Lighthouse Board

Washington , D. C.

Dear sir:

The lighthouse tender Haze is here and has taken on board the iron tower and lantern which is to be erected at Vermilion Harbor, Ohio, in place of the old wooden tower now standing there.

Office of the Lighthouse Engineer

Tenth District

Oswego, New York

August 31, 1877.

NOTES

When the Lighthouse Tender *Haze* arrived in Vermilion, as described in the next chapter, she would be moored just upriver from the then wooden pier, a few hundred feet down river from the shipbuilding activity. Vermilion was a busy seaport. Several two or three-masted schooners would be built and fitted-out each year. The vessels were launched sideways from the foot of Huron street. Spars, booms, and gaffs together with fixed and running rigging would be added after launching to make the vessel ship-shape. Rotted remains of this type gear was unearthed in the 1920s when excavating for the north extension of the town's waterworks. These elements had been fabricated in three large wooden sheds north of the foot of Huron street, structures which remained until about 1930.

At the time of the *Haze* visit this vessel building and fitting-out site at and north of the foot of Huron street possessed an iron forge. It was capable of taking bog-iron found a few miles south of Vermilion and turning it into simple iron sand castings. George Patterson Wakefield has written of this forge. And a few hundred feet north of the foundry was the limekiln being charged from thrice-weekly schooner-loads of limestone from Kelley's Island quarries, some twenty miles west by northwest from the Vermilion lighthouse. All local land-hauling was by teams of horses and wagons. Everyone was active, boys and men employed around the river; the girls helped their mothers at home. America was being built!

In addition to the larger traffic which included lumber schooners, more than a dozen fishing smacks and many fishing rowboats daily plied the river. So the port was busy for the visiting Lighthouse Tender *Haze.*

One of the shipping families at the time was that of Captain Alva Bradley, who in modern times would have a large ore-boat named after him. Captain Bradley and his family lived on Huron street just west of the Inland Seas Maritime Museum. Thomas Edison, the future inventor of the incandescent lamp (1879) who was born and lived in nearby Milan, was a close friend of the Bradleys. Even today Edison is classed as the greatest American inventor with more than one-thousand patents. Almost surely the young Edison became familiar with lake shipping as a guest of the Bradleys. Indeed, local lore has the young boys making a trip across Lake Erie to Long Point, Ontario in one of the Bradley Company schooners.

With so much vessel traffic, personnel aboard the Lighthouse Tender *Haze* soon felt Vermilion had earned the right to have a new iron lighthouse mounted on the end of the west pier.

Charles K. Hyde has authored a most interesting publication *The Northern Lights: Lighthouses of the Upper Great Lakes*, Volume VI of the Michigan Heritage Series, *Michigan Natural Resources Magazine*, Lansing, Michigan. Hyde states the *Haze* was the first steam-powered propeller vessel to act as a lighthouse tender serving from 1867 to 1905. His article contains a wealth of information on lighthouses of the area cited.

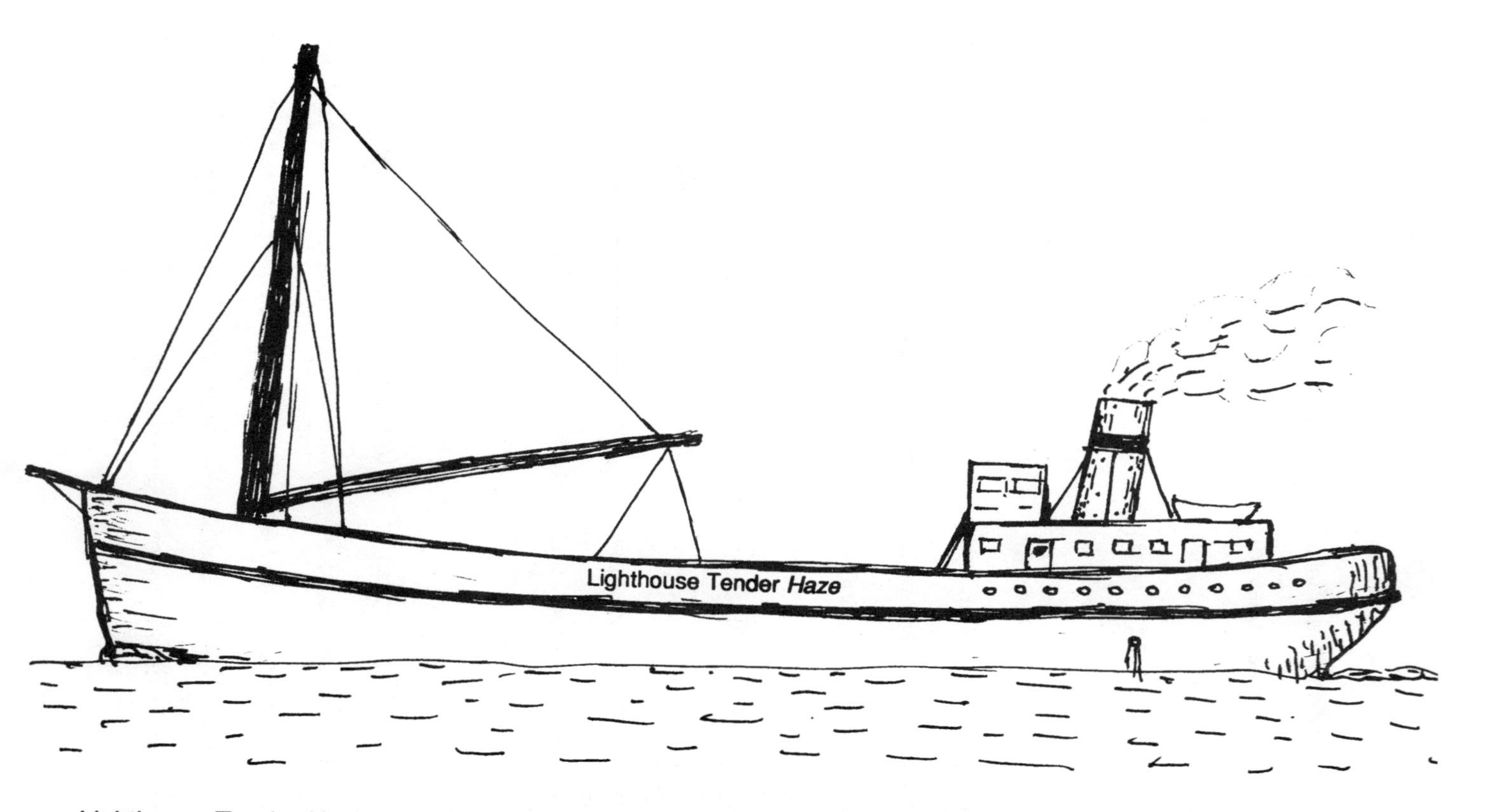

Lighthouse Tender *Haze* steaming to Oswego to load elements of the Vermilion lighthouse. Ernest H. Wakefield.

The underwater stern of a steam vessel such as the *Haze*. The Century Co., 1887.

Chapter 2

THE LIGHTHOUSE TENDER *HAZE,* & THE ERECTION OF THE 1877 VERMILION LIGHTHOUSE

The lighthouse tender *Haze* was a wood-hulled vessel measuring 150 feet in length with a beam of 22 feet. She had been built with keelson, stem piece, sternpost, and ribs of white oak hewn from the forest in the Adirondacks. Her planking was of choice white pine taken from the woods of northern Michigan. Deck support and deck planking was also of hard-surface oak to withstand the heavy parts she would regularly carry:- light buoys, lighthouse sections, oil stores, etc.

Her coal-fired boiler had been built in Buffalo. Her double expansion, two-cylinder steam-engine, constructed in Schenectady, could deliver some 200-horsepower. This engine would turn a six-foot diameter, four-blade propeller at 70 revolutions per minute to yield a speed of ten knots.

From her hull a rear deck-structure housed her crew and cooking facilities. The captain's quarters were in a smaller, second-story cabin. Forward, leaving a large open deckspace, was a derrick with winch, boom and hoisting ability. Power was supplied from a coal-fired, steam, donkey-engine. Built immediately after the Civil War, the golden-age of steam-engines and the prime source of concentrated power, the *Haze* was a lucky ship. The last spike hammered home in her transom had been of silver dug from the Comstock mine in Nevada.

With the derrick, the various elements of the 1877 Vermilion lighthouse were transferred from the canal barges to the deck of the *Haze*, and there secured.

The first day of September 1877 the *Haze* slowly steamed from the Oswego harbor bearing its precious burden and headed westward for Port Dalhousie, Ontario, Canada. This port is the Lake Ontario entrance to the Canadian Welland Canal. It was opened in 1829, and links this lower lake to the higher level, 326 feet, Lake Erie. Between the two bodies lies the Niagara Falls and the swift flowing Niagara river.

In 1877, after a canal restructuring in 1845, a series of twenty-seven locks raised the *Haze* to the water level of Port Colborne, the Lake Erie end of the Welland Canal. Again gapers from farm and town too viewed the disassembled lighthouse.

ERECTION OF THE 1877 VERMILION LIGHTHOUSE

From this port, before steaming on Lake Erie to Vermilion to the west, the *Haze* would call at Cleveland Harbor, and there pick up the erection crew for placing the lighthouse on the pier at Vermilion. Here lumber for forms and lime would be placed aboard for building the lighthouse foundation. Sand and gravel would be procured locally in Vermilion. In addition, the secured box containing the Fresnel lens, and the light source, a whale-oil-burning lantern was also loaded.

On a late summer day after a day's run from Cleveland the *Haze* pulled into the Vermilion river and moored at the south end of the wooden pier. There stood a large shed, later to be owned by Thomas Ball. In this structure were fashioned such wooden elements as keels, ribs, stems, deck beams, spars, booms, and whisker poles for two and three-masted schooners built at the foot of Huron street. A little removed was a forge for fashioning eye-bolts, iron-sections, and where anchors might be cast from wrought iron, etc. Canvas sails for the schooners were cut, sewn, roped and brass-grommeted in a sail loft farther upriver. Ropes and cordage, of hemp from India, would come from the East. Cables for the schooners had as its source the steel mills of Cleveland.

Within a few days the lighthouse erection crew had bolted together wooden forms and, using additional lime from the nearby limekiln, and sand and gravel from the beach, had constructed a strong foundation for the new 1877 Vermilion Lighthouse.

On a day when the lake was smooth, and in September there are many such days on Lake Erie, the *Haze* steamed from the dock and moored beside the pier where the lighthouse would be erected. The derrick aboard the *Haze* lifted the lower ring of cast-iron and, guided by the men, was bolted to the foundation of the lighthouse. Successively the tapering rings were lifted into position and bolted to each other. Then the pediment was placed, and finally the lantern. Installed later was the scientifically sculpted and carefully packed Fresnel lens and the oil light source. This delicate series of circular prisms, one on top of another, and fastened in a cast brass frame, channel the spherically emitted light from the burning wick to issue in a direction whose plane is parallel to the lake surface. Thus a vessel could more readily see, and at a greater distance, the red lighthouse-beam which marked the Vermilion Harbor. Finally the lantern would be glazed. Later, immediately south of the lighthouse a 540-gallon capacity steel oil-shed was erected in 1906 as seen on the cover of this book.

From 1877 to 1929 this light was a sentinel for lake voyagers. The light regularly was attended by the faithful lighthouse keeper who, in addition to the tasks cited above, regularly polished the many glass prisms of the Fresnel lens. Only when the lake navigation was closed was the lighthouse shuttered. For fifty-two years the sentinel offered a safe haven to commercial ships, both sail and steam, fishermen and yachtsmen.

In the 1890s Cleveland yachtmen discovered Vermilion was thirty miles from their Lakewood Yacht Club in Rocky River. It was a convenient rendezvous for their weekend sail races. Later the Lakewood Yacht Club would become the Cleveland Yachting Club. It was through sailing his sloop *Unique III* that Commodore Frederick William Wakefield learned of the town. With his later *Lotus*, the first gasoline-powered yacht in Cleveland, he would regularly visit Vermilion. Gasoline in that period had an octane rating of 40, and engines were cranky. In 1906 he would move his factory, The F. W. Wakefield Brass Company, to Vermilion. In 1909 he had built his *Harbor View* from gravel shovelled from the lake. This home became the original structure of the Inland Seas Marine Museum.

About the turn of the century the limekiln fell into disuse. No longer was its lime mortar able to compete with manufactured cement, a calcareous material forming a better and more lasting bond with brick. Only in 1915 was the kiln's great iron stack pulled down under the jurisdiction of Albert Frederick Wakefield. It was a means of providing scrap-iron for helping the World War I war effort, an event in which he and other Vermilionites would later participate in France. And as late as the 1930s the Wakefield boys: Frederick Wright, George Patterson, Theodore, and Ernest Henry used sandstone from the base of the kiln to rebuild the river dock just north of the foot of Huron street.

CHANGING CARGOES ON THE VERMILION RIVER

The passing of the 18th Amendment to the U. S. Constitution would have a profound effect on vessel passages in the Vermilion river. Few, if any, Vermilionites foresaw the results. What had earlier been limestone, lime, iron castings,

By 1900 the once busy Vermilion port had dwindled only to fishing boats. Then it was "discovered" by Cleveland yachtsmen. "The skipper at the left is my father, Frederick W. Wakefield, who sailed his sloop the *Unique III* in the race to Vermilion (September 7, 1903)." George P. Wakefield (Photo: Pearl Roscoe).

The 1877 light as seen from *Harbor View* in1922. Theodore D. Wakefield.

lumber and fish cargoes plying the river, the prohibition of making and distilling alcoholic liquors in the United States would cause the Vermilion river to be an important entry point for Canadian liquors. And this illicit trade would be participated in by many citizens of the town.

Fish boats regularly completed a round trip to Canada and entered the harbor in broad daylight. So brazen did this passage become that even after a 75-foot coast-guard vessel was assigned to Vermilion two rum-running boats were cornered on the beach immediately before the Inland Seas Maritime Museum. In attempting to escape, bundles of contraband were jettisoned into the shallow water only to be claimed by waders the next morning. George Wakefield in Appendix C and Karen Cornelius in Appendix D relate stories of Vermilion rum-runners.

REMOVAL OF THE 1877 VERMILION LIGHTHOUSE

In the summer of 1929 teenage brothers Theodore and Ernest Wakefield, playing tag with others on the west pier, noted the 1877 light was tipping toward the river. They were cognizant enough with maritime matters to know the danger.

"Let's tell Dad," one told the other.

Dad, the old Commodore Frederick William Wakefield, (1863-1934), on hearing this news, lighted his cigar and with his two sons, joined by a third, George, walked from their home *Harbor View*. Down to the river and out the pier the foursome trod, the equivalent of two city blocks, to more carefully examine the lighthouse.

"Sure enough," exclaimed the old Commodore to his sons, "this light may topple into the river. We must immediately notify the U. S. Lighthouse Service in Cleveland."

The very next day two Corps Engineers came to Vermilion on the electric trolley, called on the Commodore, and together the three, followed by the three sons tread the pier to examine the lighthouse.

"Yes, we must repair this light immediately. Let us return

and alert the tug boat captain and the crew of the derrick-barge," said the older engineer.

Within a week a U.S. Corps of Engineer steam tug, a derrick-bearing barge, and a block-stone carrying scow appeared before the harbor, and proceeded to lay at the same dock the *Haze* had lain to in 1877.

When the lake was smooth the men of the derrick-barge carefully disassembled the lighthouse so skillfully erected fifty-two years earlier. The steam derrick barge *Erie* carried out this task. In place of the attractive 1877 Vermilion lighthouse seen on the cover of this book an austere steel-tower, steep-sided and truncated pyramid was erected to the laments of the local citizens. True, this new structure continued to bear a red light, but as it was automatically controlled no lighthouse keeper was required. The beacon had little charm and less nostalgia.

The little lighthouse that could was no more!

The old Commodore offered to purchase the 1877 Vermilion lighthouse from the U. S. Government to be erected on his grounds. Indeed, the tug and barge were lying at his dock. But it was not to be. Where this lighthouse was taken is unknown as reported to T. D. Wakefield by John A. Dwyer, Cartographic & Architectural Branch of the U. S. National Archives.

More than sixty years passed.

The old Commodore was long in his grave. Commercial fishing from early sailing craft, later steam tugs, and later still, gasoline-powered fishboats in Lake Erie were but a memory, as was the entry of liquor-laden fishing boats, the results of the 21st Amendment to the U. S. Constitution. Sport fishing only flourished. The lake was now a paradise for sport fishermen and women. Walleyed pike of 10 and 15 pounds were the trophies. The harbor instead of being filled with net-casting fishing boats was now almost choked with yachts from small skiffs to ketches, yawls and powerful diesel cruisers. Affluence was everywhere. At the dock where the *Haze* had moored in 1877, on a summer weekend a one-hundred and fifty-thousand dollar yacht would pass every twenty seconds! And the river had only a width across which a tall boy could fling a stone. With all this activity, strangely, flotillas of ducks, genetically remembering their Vermilion river of the Indians, still are commonly seen dodging the river traffic.

North of the pierhead now lies the detached breakwater built by the Federal Government to ease the entry of vessels in the Vermilion river in vicious, northeast storms. This steel-walled, tall to prevent seas from breaking over it, inaccessible island both to seagull egg-eating rats and fisherman is now the safe home to thousands of silver-white gulls, *Larus Argentatus.* and *Argentus Delawarensis.* Recently local personnel, interested in lengthening the tourist season by establishing bird-watching meetings, have discovered this outer breakwater has been occupied by rare, Great Black-backed Gulls, *Larus Marinus.* These immense gulls, normally seen in the Labrador, Nova Scotia area, can have a length of as much as 32 inches, and add to the charm of the Vermilion river region.

Notes

After the 1877 Vermilion lighthhouse was operating a number of notable vessels visited the port. Among them was the luxurious yacht *La Belle*. As William F. Rapprich writes in *A Memorable Yacht: From Halcyon Days To Holocaust.*

"The story of the *La Belle* starts in the fall of 1909 when Commodore Alexander Winton, builder of the Winton automobile (the *Winton* had been the first to be driven across the United States), negotiated with Cox & Stevens, noted naval architects of New York, to design a motor yacht second to none on the Great Lakes. The following year a contract was entered into with John H. Dialogue & Sons of Camden, New Jersey, for the construction of this vessel.

"In 1911 the *La Belle* was launched, fitted out and delivered to her home port of Rocky River, Ohio via the St. Lawrence river and Welland Canal. Miss Agnes Winton, daughter of the owner, christened the ship *La Belle* in honor of the owner's wife, and the beautiful yacht slid down the ways. This stately vessel was built of steel, measuring 145 feet overall excluding the bowsprit, 129 feet keel length, clipper bow and fantail stern, 19.1 feet in beam and a molded depth of 9.7 feet. Her gross tonnage was 165 tons, 112 net tons, and she held Official U.S. Registry No. 208,565.

"Commodore Winton built the engines for the *La Belle* in his plant in Cleveland. She was powered by three 6-cylinder engines, 8 1/2-inch diameter by 11-inch stroke, developing 175 horsepower each at 500 revolutions per minute, producing a speed of 13 miles per hour.

"The initial voyage from Camden, New Jersey, to Rocky River was under the Commodore's command...."

In August 1911 Commodore & Mrs. Winton aboard their yacht *La Belle* entered the Vermilion harbor to pay a courtesy call on Commodore & Mrs. F. W. Wakefield, the latter having preceded Winton as commodore of the Lakewood Yacht Club, later renamed the Cleveland Yachting Club. The *La Belle* was the largest yacht ever to enter Vermilion harbor. The *La Belle*, after changing hands several times and reduced to a vessel carrying fuel to island dwellers in Lakes Michigan and Superior, struck a reef in the latter waters. Abandoned, much of the fuel was siphoned out. Then she burned. The *La Belle* was scrapped in Detroit in 1943 to provide iron for the war effort.

A word is warranted about Alexander Winton of whom no biography is known to exist. Winton, a Cleveland resident, was a mechanical genius. At the turn of the century his gasoline-powered automobile, the *Winton,* was a competitor to Henry Ford's automobiles. Alexander, indeed, at the wheel of his motorcar raced Ford and lost. Inasmuch as the Winton company was an integrated factory he chose for development a less competitive field and introduced into America from Germany Dr.

Rudolf Diesel's 1897-invented engine of the same name.[1] In the early 1900s inasmuch as Kaiser Wilhelm II was intent on overtaking England for world domination he encouraged his navy chiefs to develop the submarine. Germany had great competency in three important areas for submarines: electric batteries, motor/generators for driving vessels while underwater, and the diesel engine. Gasoline engines are inappropriate for submarine use for the fuel is too volatile for the closed environment of an underwater boat. German submarines, as is known, almost brought England to its knees in the 1914-18 war (and again in World War II).

Winton, realizing the high efficiency of the diesel engine and its ability to burn a variety of fuels, initiated the production of diesel engines in his Cleveland plant, and proceeded to equip all American submarines in World War I. Later, Winton initiated the first diesel railroad locomotive. Subsequently the Winton Diesel Engine Company was purchased from the Winton family by the General Motors Corporation. The company was moved to Chicago to become the GM Electromotive Works which, with other companies, made diesel railroad engines universal prime movers on railroads almost all over the world.

Besides the *La Belle* three other notable vessels entered the port of Vermilion: The *Sophie Minch*, the *George B. King*, and the *Vermilion of Vermilion.*

---

1. In 1913 Rudolph Diesel, at the apogee of his acclaim, was lost at sea while crossing the England Channel, a mystery which has never been solved.

The *Sophie Minch* arrived in the middle 1920s. She was a three-masted schooner bearing pontoons, now reduced to a barge. Towed to Vermilion she had had her starboard-quarter bow smashed in a collision. She was moored at the foot of Huron street, occupying a good share of the river. The vessel would be repaired by the yet-living schooner ship-carpenters: Tom Ball, Jim Brooks, and others. Soon made nearly new the *Sophie Minch* was again towed out to carry trade goods.

Whereas the above had been a sailing vessel the *George B. King* was a wooden-hulled steamer whose boiler room and aft section had been burned out. She very closely resembled the *Harvey J. Kendall* shown in the illustration. Of these two vessel the author, his brothers and others, like water rats, were all over the ships from the cargo holds to the cabins. And from their superstructure these 'teenagers would dive into the river. Repaired, the *King* again entered the lumber and coal-carrying trade where her diminutive size would enable her to enter the many small harbors bounding the lakes.

A vessel which came into the Vermilion river every other day in the 1920s was the *Vermilion of Vermilion.* She was of a class of vessel known as a sandsucker and was owned by a remarkable local man, Captain Edward Lampe. The *Vermilion*, a wooden-hulled vessel built in Vermilion, bore a small pilot-house forward. The balance of the deck space was open with fencing at the edges. On this large area the sand was placed. According to Peter Smith, her engineer, she bore twenty-two gasoline engines. Six were used for forward and reverse while the others pumped sand from the lake bottom, served as hose-lifting equipment, powered the fire-fighting equipment, operated the winches for the anchors, etc. Every other day the *Vermilion* would leave port, head due north for six miles, anchor, and pump sand from the lake bottom for some 12 to 14 hours. Wives of the crew members could see the vessel on the horizon knowing they were safe even though removed. Likewise they could witness when the vessel up-anchored and headed for home. Fish boats, on the other hand, set their nets usually farther from the port and were invisible to shore-based people.

Arriving in port the *Vermilion of Vermilion* would lay at the foot of Huron street where a land-based derrick would unload the sand, piling it on the street-end. In the 1920s there was a bull market for sand. The nation was alive with the building of concrete roads for Americans had fallen in love with the motorcar. A brand new Ford automobile could be purchased for $245.00. Captain Lampe had been a fisherman operating the Lampe Fisheries from a covey of structures upriver from the Route 2 bridge. One of his steam fishboats was named *Mary and John*, after his two children. She was the only steam fishing boat in the harbor to bear twin smoke-stacks.

The above unique vessels were somewhat of an aberrant. The characteristic sounds of the Vermilion port in the 1920s were the soft coming and goings of the seven or eight steam fishing vessels, the noisy exhaust of the trapnet boats, the singing whine of the racks as the gill nets were being wound for drying, the sharp cry of gulls and terns when a school of minnows had been sighted, the hollow whistle-hoot of the sometime hurrying trains, the splash of a mallard duck alighting. At the site of the

the 1877 Vermilion Lighthouse there was only the wash of the incoming waves on the mossy sandstone pier-blocks. Near nature there are long periods of silence.

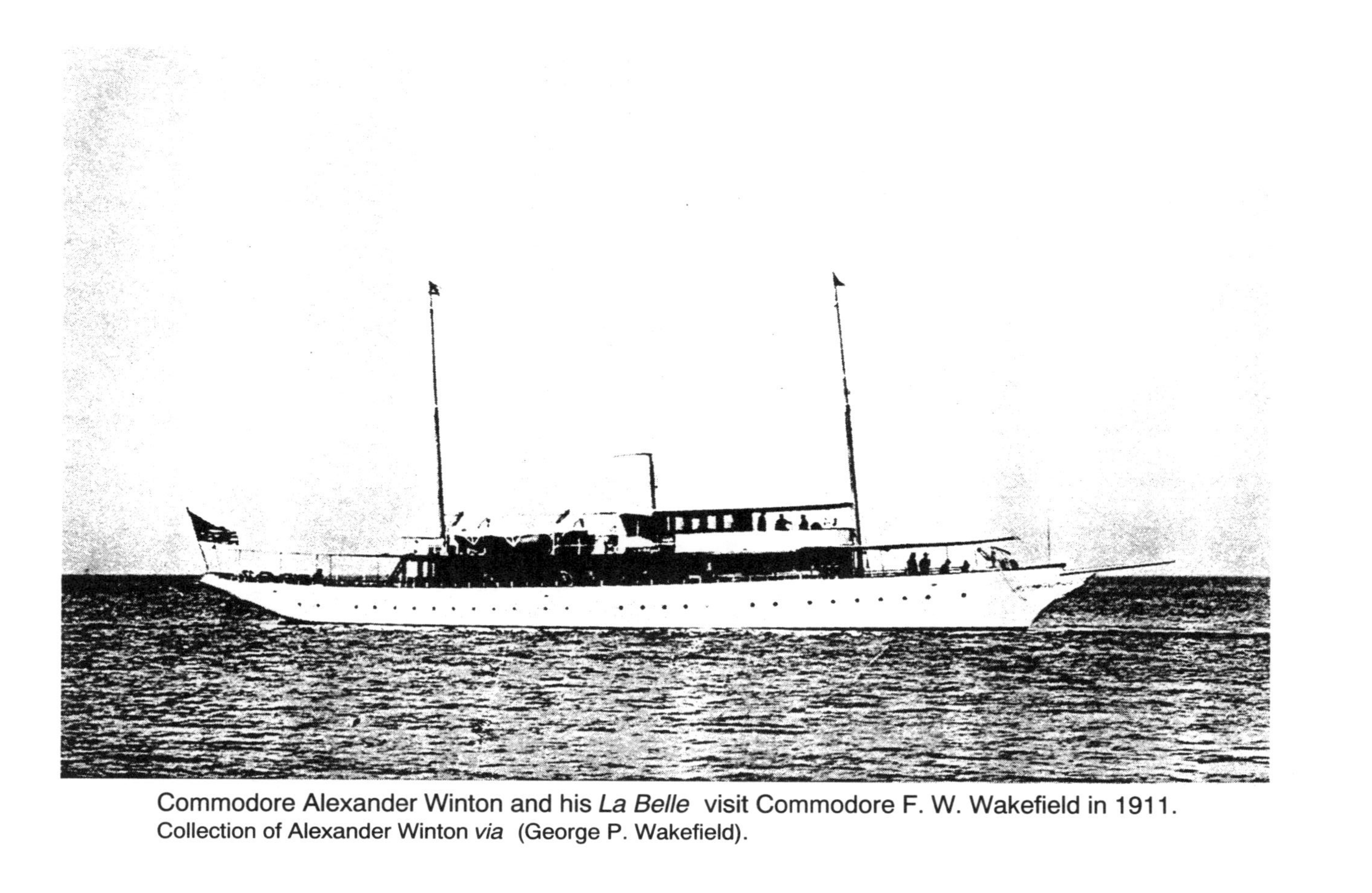

Commodore Alexander Winton and his *La Belle* visit Commodore F. W. Wakefield in 1911.
Collection of Alexander Winton *via* (George P. Wakefield).

Chapter 3

PLANNING THE REPLICA OF THE 1877 LIGHTHOUSE AND ITS ERECTION

Commodore Frederick W. Wakefield's *Harbor View*, a poured-concrete, vine-covered home, on the death of his widow, was given to the Great Lakes Historical Society. Trustees of this organization turned its spacious quarters into a maritime museum. Albert Frederick Wakefield, the old Commodore's eldest son, had contributed a wing to the museum.

Now Theodore "Ted" Wakefield, the ninth child of the Commodore, himself now long retired, daily looked from his lake and riverside-home window, beside the dock where in September 1877 lay the Lighthouse Tender *Haze*. He would dream of the classic 1877 Vermilion lighthouse which earlier marked the quaint fishing port of the town in which he was born. Ted had already been the driving force for creating the *Harbour Town 1837* in the village center, thus encouraging all downtown buildings to maintain their 19th century appearance.

Harbor View the year it was donated to the Great Lakes Historical Society. Albert F. Wakefield.

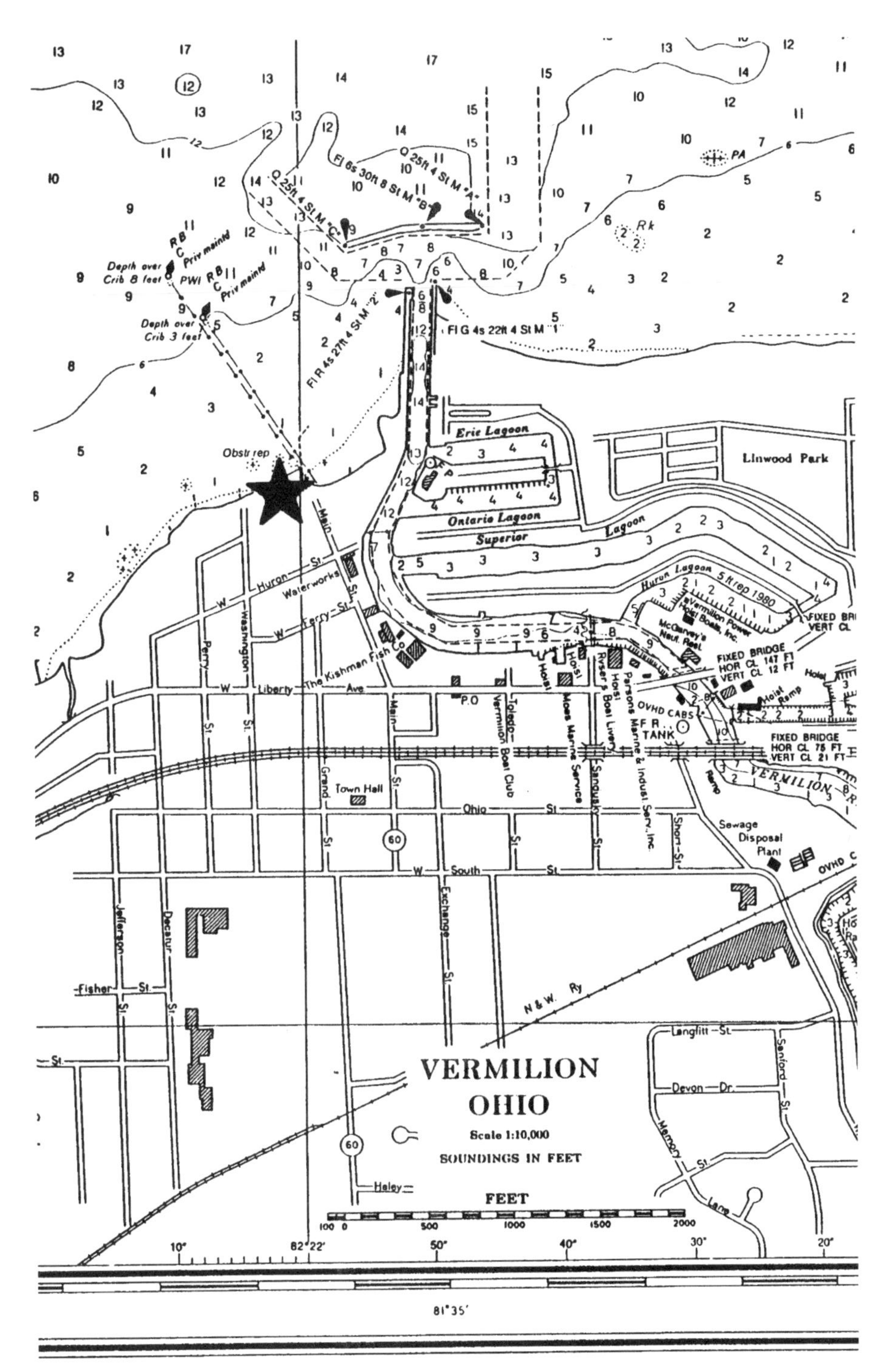

The star orients the Museum on an 1989 chart. Theodore D. Wakefield.

"Why not," he querried his retired psychiatrist wife Margaret, after sighting the harbor entrance for perhaps the 3,000th time, "Why not try to raise funds and erect a replica of the 1877 Vermilion lighthouse and place it besides the old homestead now part of the Inland Seas Maritime Museum?"

Margaret showed great interest. So did brother George who, also retired, had become the harbor's historian writing for both the *Inland Seas*, the journal of the Great Lakes Historical Society, and a weekly maritime column in the *Vermilion Photojournal*. Interest was found as well among the Museum Trustees.

So began the interminable planning. An architect was engaged, Robert Lee Tracht of nearby Huron. Plans were drawn for an exact replica of the 1877 Vermilion lighthouse, seen in the attached Figure. The design was approved by the city, county, state authorities, but only after almost interminable delay. Even the U. S. Coast Guard, guardians of nautical markers on federal navigable waters, approved the plans for

Lighthouse model

A model of what the replica lighthouse will look like is on display at Society Bank, Vermilion, courtesy of George Mayer, president.

Photojournal: Wally Wheatley.

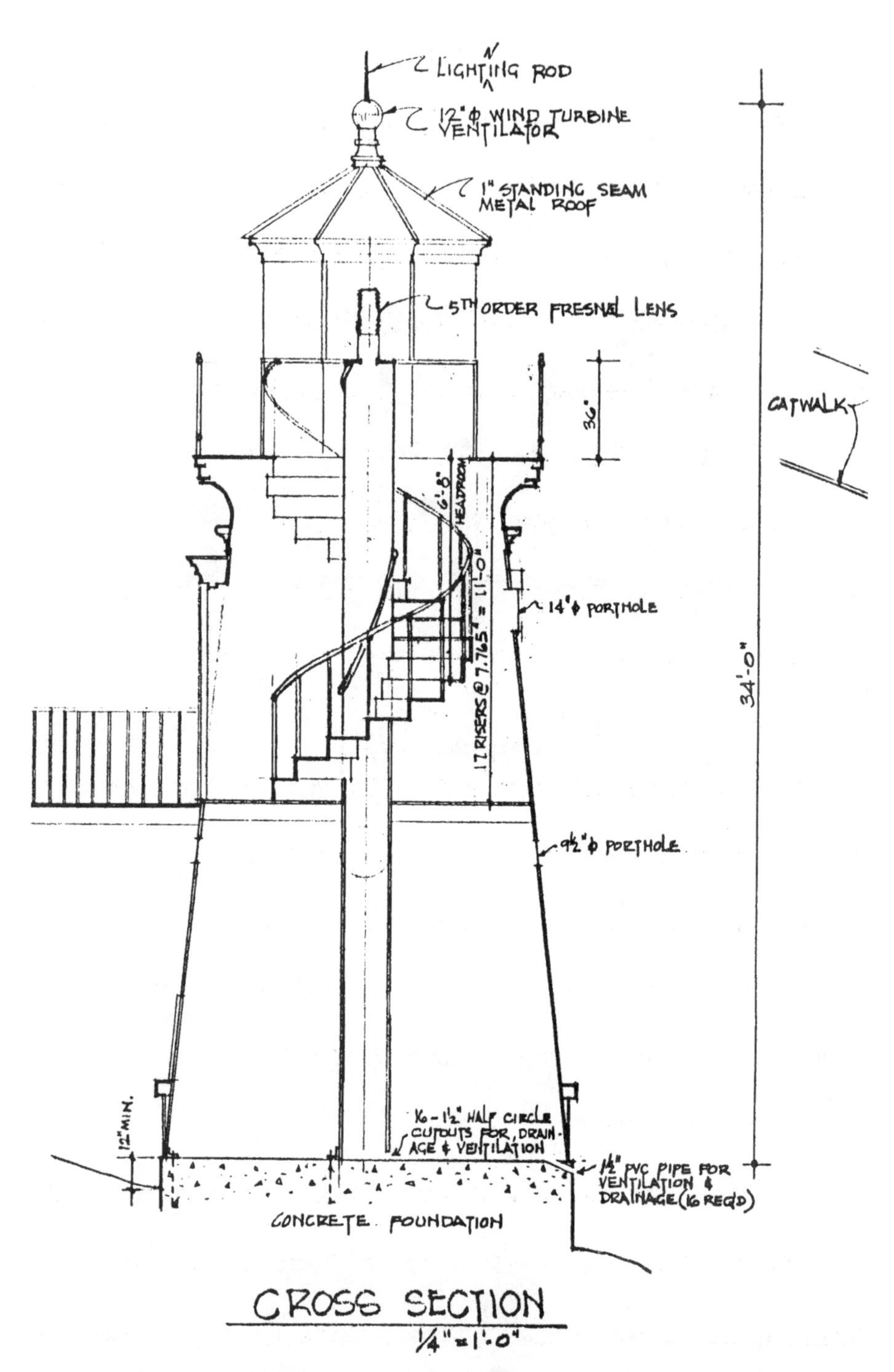

Elevation: Replica Vermilion Lighthouse. Robert L. Tracht.

making the light a working lighthouse, even to bearing the historical steady red light. This approval came through the good offices of William Craig, Aid to Navigation, Ninth Coast Guard District, Cleveland. The 1877 Vermilion lighthouse replica, he promised, would be placed on navigational charts.

FUND RAISING FOR THE REPLICA

The town's shakers and movers joined in. The local media was enthusiastic. Karen Cornelius, Editor of the *Vermilion Photojournal* wrote numerous articles, while Wally Wheatley, the paper's photographer, furnished many photographs. Funds were raised by mailing a brochure with contained self-addressed envelopes to some 2500 names of persons, companies, and institutions. More than 500 responded. A sum in excess of sixty-two thousand dollars was collected. Helping to reach this total were small donations received from daily attendees of the Museum.

With plans for the replica completed, contracts were let. Just as in 1876 a steel company in Buffalo assembled the lighthouse for Vermilion to the satisfaction of Professor

Vermilion leader Ted Wakefield points to financial goal.
Vermilion Photojournal: Wally Wheatley.

Steering committee for replica lighthouse: Howard H. Baxter, John L. Reulbach, Alexander B. Cook, Theodore D. Wakefield.
Vermilion Photojournal: Wally Wheatley.

Vermilion Mayor Alex Angney breaking ground.
Photojournal: Wally Wheatley.

Joseph Henry, so did the Milan Fabricators of the Roth Manufacturing Company in the Huron river valley of Milan, Ohio begin fabricating an exact replica to the satisfaction of the architect. While no picture is known for those men who constructed the first lighthouse, illustrations are enclosed of the architect, named above, Klaus H. Bauer, President of Roth Manufacturing Company whose company assumed the replica lighthouse contract, as well as the actual builders of the 1877 Vermilion lighthouse replica.

On 24 July 1991 Mayor Alex Angney of Vermilion moved the first shovel of earth for the new lighthouse concrete foundation at the site of the Inland Seas Maritime Museum. Cameras clicked.

The architectural plans for the foundation of the replica lighthouse excavation, which the mayor began, called for a hole sixteen-feet in diameter and twelve-feet deep. A casing was provided, which when inserted, allowed a fifteen-foot diameter octagon of concrete to be poured. Did the operator of the back-hoe which did the digging realize this was Indian camping land that was being dug?

The old Commodore in 1909, when observing the clay piles which resulted from digging the foundation for the original building of the museum, his *Harbor View,* had found two artifacts of historical interest. One, a perfectly chipped three-inch arrow-head, of light orange quartzite. He had rubbed it free of clay, then pocketed while continuing the inspection of his new home-to-be. Later, when the main body of the house was constructed, and the walk to the foot of Main street was being completed he inserted his chipped-arrow into the fresh concrete in the north curb, immediately east of porch steps. For many years this arrow-head glistened in the daylight, and even in the darkness, to sharp eyes, it gleamed. With the old Commodore's death, and with his absence noticed, a vandal who undoubtedly long knew of this treasure, chipped-out with a hammer and cold-chisel this talisman. The ghoul left his handiwork, a depression which to this day is visible. To the old Commodore, respect in life, affront in death.

The site wherein sits the Inland Seas Marine Museum the old Commodore always believed was a site of a small Indian village. In that early time when eagles yet nested in tall, noble sycamore trees along the banks, the river outlet was at the foot of the Museum hill. If one today stands on the entrance porch of this marine collection and views the east end of the walk-way leading to the Museum, the depressed lake-end of Main street was, for a short time, the old river bed. Beyond, the land is seen to rise forming the opposite bank of the river. From this rise, the land again slopes downward leading eventually to the present river bed.

The current stream has not always held to its channel, even in historical memory. In 1906 the river cut a channel to the lake exactly where the present home of Ted Wakefield stands.

When that area was indeed fallow and rabbits there burrowed, a deep basin, always seeped with water, was present. Frog eggs could be found in the spring of the year when the robins had returned, dandelions bloomed, and lilac gave forth their heaven-sent odors. To minimize the possibility of the river again cutting a new channel the then short west pier was extended some 300 feet upriver by the U. S. Corps of Engineers, terminating at its present south end.

When in 1968 eleven inches of rain fell in the watershed of the Vermilion river and the stream filled such that it flowed both under and over the Vermilion river bridge at McGarvey's restaurant, the deluge again cut through Ted Wakefield's land, carrying away part of his home! Nature in the raw is seldom mild!

The second artifact found by the old Commodore in the clay dug up from the foundation of his home was a pair of wrought-iron, prisoner leg-irons. Because they were of wrought-iron, they were untouched by time, gleaming charcoal and silver from their menacing use. For many years this remnant of the past hung from a candle-light holder screwed to the plastered wall in the Commodore's den. It still can be seen in the rare book section of the Museum. Had this site, after the Indians moved west beyond reach of the trans-gressing white man, been a convenient location for temporarily housing some of the British sailors captured by Commodore Oliver Hazard Perry in the Battle of Lake Erie in 1812?

When the back-hoe, digging for the foundation of the light-house replica, stabbed its teeth into this favored soil, this Indian hallowed-ground, this remnant of the War of 1812, what rare archival materials might have been over-looked?

ERECTION OF THE REPLICA OF THE 1877 LIGHT

The fabricated base of the lighthouse was transported from Milan to Vermilion by a low-bodied truck, as was the lantern in a second conveyance. Cranes, coordinated by local erector Randy Strauss, first picked-up the assembled octahedral base and carefully lowered it onto the previously poured

Lighthouse base lowered on flat-bed truck.
M. R. Wakefield.

Easing out the fabricating plant.
M. R. Wakefield.

Fabricators kiss their favorite job goodbye.
M. R. Wakefield.

Leaving Milan on way to Vermilion.
M. R. Wakefield.

foundation. All fit perfectly. The next day the lantern was lowered onto the base. Just as the townspeople and visitors cheer the erection of the lighthouse in 1877, so did a group of local and distant citizens, more than a century later, applaud the erection of the replica in 1991.

It has been rumored that an early resident of Vermilion, at the scene, gave an 1877 one-ounce goldpiece to a volunteer rigger. He place it on the foundation at that vertex of the octahedron that points true north. Adding credence to the story is the accompanying illustration. The arm of a rigger is clearly seen under the lighthouse base as it was being lowered onto the foundation. If true, the 1877 Vermilion lighthouse replica is melded to the good earth of Vermilion through the noble metal of gold.

The interior of the lighthouse was electrically wired. Subsequently another Fresnel lens, owned by the Museum, similar to the one of 1877, was securely mounted. This lens is

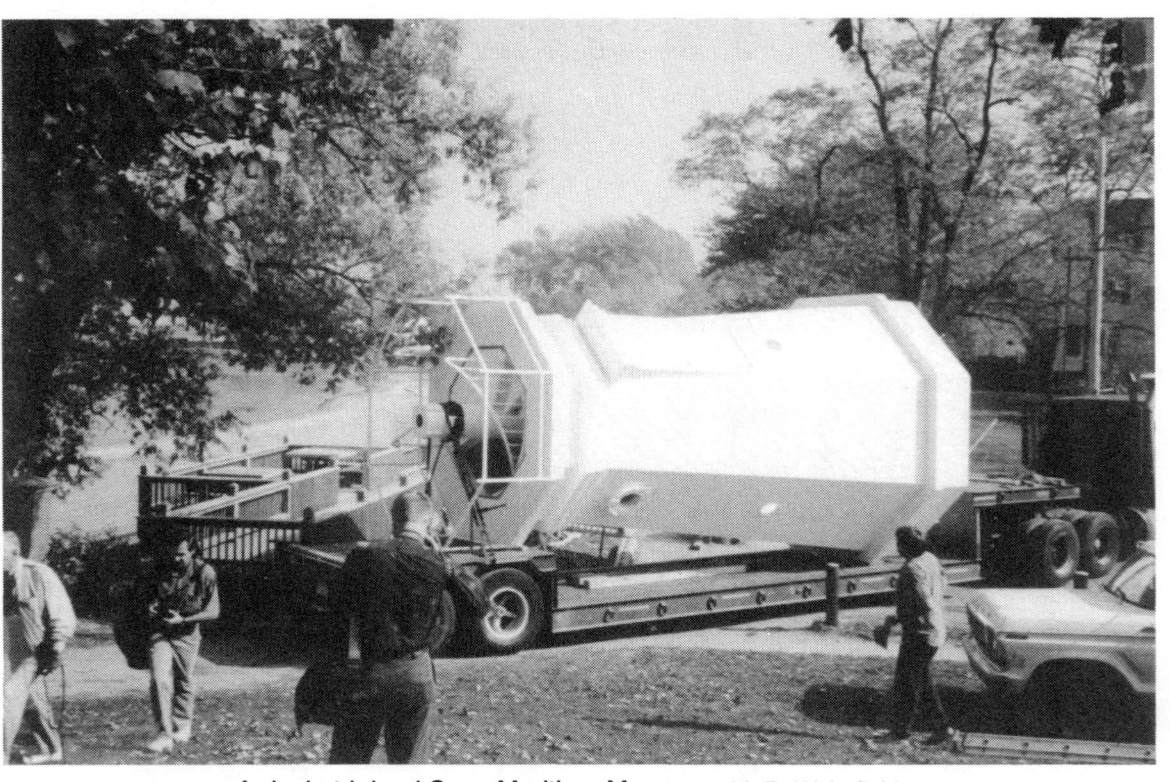

Arrival at Inland Seas Maritime Museum. M. R. Wakefield.

In less than three hours' time, the lighthouse was raised on the site of the Inland Seas Maritime Museum overlooking Lake Erie on Wednesday, October 23, 1991. Cranes hoist the 25,000 pound lighthouse base off the flatbed truck used to transport the steel-plated structure from Milan Fabricators. Vermilion Photojournal. Wally Wheatley.

Vermilion resident Randy Strauss, volunteer construction manager, crawls under the 11-ton plus lighthouse to check that the holes will line up with the bolts before swinging the lighthouse over its foundation. Crane operators Keith and Richard Decker of Crane Rental Service Services, Inc. of Sandusky, donated their expertise anchoring the lighthouse. *Cleveland Plain Dealer*, 26 December 1991: Ramon Owen.

Staircase to Fresnel lens and light source.
Photojournal: Wally Wheatley.

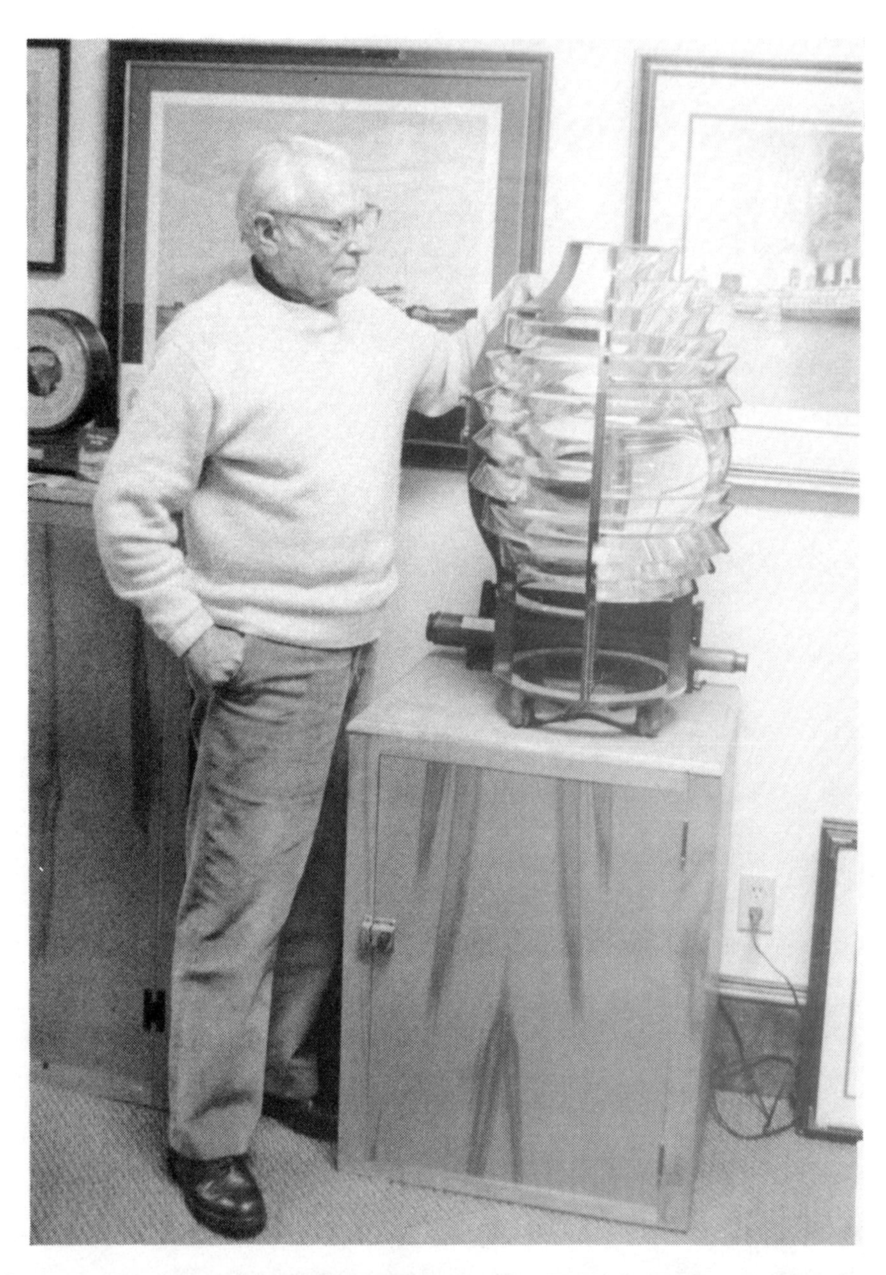

Our own "Vermilion Views" Historian George P. Wakefield examines the Fresnel lens which will be used in the lighthouse reconstruction. Wakefield is a member of the Great Lakes Historical Society whose museum is housed in his former family home. (Photojournal photo - Wally Wheatley)

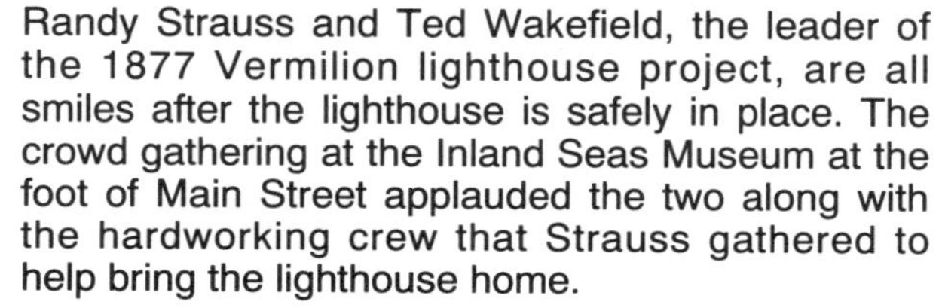

Randy Strauss and Ted Wakefield, the leader of the 1877 Vermilion lighthouse project, are all smiles after the lighthouse is safely in place. The crowd gathering at the Inland Seas Museum at the foot of Main Street applauded the two along with the hardworking crew that Strauss gathered to help bring the lighthouse home.

Putting the icing on the cake so to speak is a crew from Beaver Park North who came with another crane on Thursday, October 24, to mount the lantern and lighthouse roof.

Writing credit: Karen Cornelius
Photographs: Wally Wheatley.

shown with George Wakefield standing beside it to give a measure of its size. An incandescent lamp with Edison-base was inserted within the Fresnel assembly. To cast a red beam over the waters a transparent red glass cylinder surrounds the 200-watt clear glass lamp.

Now, from an elevation above Lake Erie's shore, a welcome light to visitors gleams, a source made possible by gifts from many people, companies, and institutions, both in cash and in kind. It was truly a community effort.

As the Log Book Supplement of the Inland Seas Maritime Museum reads: "The classic 1877-1929 Vermilion lighthouse has been duplicated and now stands on the lakefront grounds of the Inland Seas Maritime Museum, southwest of the original west pierhead site. The 34-foot high octagonal pyramidal design has been reproduced with great precision for historical accuracy. The lantern will contain a fifth-order Fresnel lens displaying a fixed red light. The lantern will be painted black, the tower white, and the base a reddish brown. The light will be operational for the opening of the 1992 navigational season, March 15th. Theodore D. Wakefield."

An exact replica of the Vermilion 1877 Lighthouse is again our sentinel.

It is *The Lighthouse That Wanted to Stay Lit*.

Century Co., 1887

Back again in all its splendor to stand guard over Vermilion's shores is the Replica 1877 Lighthouse. *Photojournal:* Wally Wheatley plus an artist.

Klaus H. Bauer, President.
Roth Manufacturing Co.
Klaus H. Bauer.

Randy K. Strauss, President
Strauss General Contracting Co.
Randy K. Strauss

Robert Lee Tracht, Architect.
Huron, Ohio
R. L. Tracht.

Joseph Whelan, Lighthouse Project Mgr. Timothy Barker, Process Eng. Klaus H. Bauer.

Lighthouse fabricators L. to R.: Bernie Mesenberg, Plant Supt., Bob Schenck, Keith Rogers, Randy Bretz, Ken Downing, Ken Neely, Randy Hall, Rick Fritz. Klaus H. Bauer.

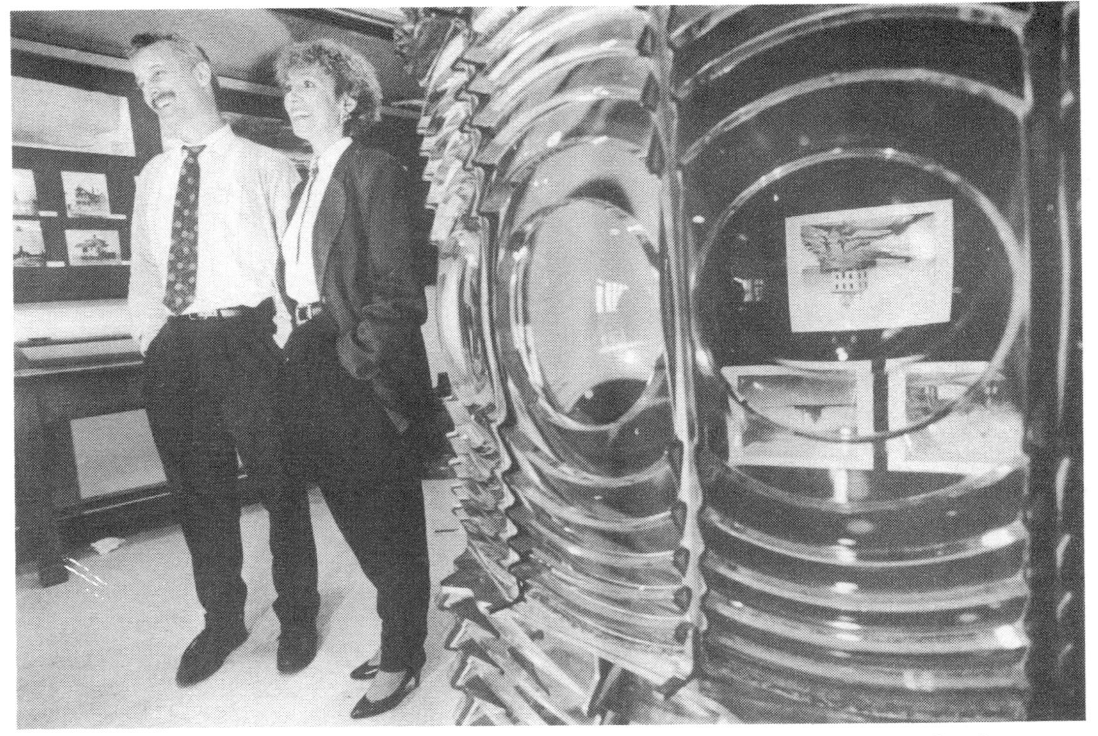

Erik and Judy Plato, caretakers of the museum. Note the upside down reflections of nearby pictures of lighthouses in Fresnel lens.
Plain Dealer, 26 Dec. 1991: Ramon Owens.

Notes

To a visitor to Vermilion who was familiar with the port in the 1920s the great differences are: the presence of the pier parallel to the shore and the accompanying thousands of gulls who call this outcropping home; the present diminutive lighthouse on the west pier instead of the nostalgic 1877 Vermilion lighthouse; the substitution of the once muskrat filled great marsh on the east side of the river with the Lagoon development; the installation of homes where before stood the schooner-building sheds and the limekiln; the replacement of the fishery houses by condominiums or yachting facilities; and the superabundant number of pleasure boats large and small. In 1920 there were two yachts in the Vermilion harbor: Commodore Tom Ball's *Iona*, and Commodore Frederick W. Wakefield's *Tobermory*.

From Lake Erie how has the harbor and the environs changed? On the weekend surely swimming in the river today would be hazardous. Boat traffic is too heavy. Lazy fishing from the pier with a bamboo pole dangling a hook bearing a wiggling worm hoping for catfish would appear unlikely. Again the many pleasure craft. Casting and spinning for white bass? Yes, if one leaves the river mouth and goes east or west and hugs the shore. Sailing on a gentle afternoon? Fine if one leaves the shore well behind. Again the crush of hook and line fishing boats.

In the 1920s when sailing on the lake with a silent off-shore breeze one might look landward and witness a lengthy low-lying dark cloud hugging the railroad tracks — the smoke of the New York Central *Commodore Vanderbilt* express train pulled by a coal-fired engine speeding through town at sixty miles per hour. There might be a second section from Chicago racing five minutes after the first. Five minutes later would be the first section of the *20th Century Limited* bearing its blue rear-borne emblem. Chicago to New York: neither boarding nor discharging passengers. A through train - 15 1/2 hours. Maybe again a second section. From the water one could see the pall of smoke left by these select trains. No more. The Chicago to New York airplanes leave their clean contrails six miles up.

And a train whistling heard from the lake? These sounds could only be lightly sensed in the silent stillness. If white steam from their blowing could be seen and the whistle heard in five-seconds, then one knew the distance off-shore to be one mile. If a ten-second interval - two miles off shore. And if one observed in the water floating paper cups and plates, a skipper would realize he was five miles off shore, the Cedar Point - Cleveland path of the cruise ship *Goodtime,* and the passenger's sad means of disposing of waste. If, instead of being at sea, one stood on the pierhead beside the proud 1877 light one would see an oncoming wave, like a line of hand clasp and laughing children, approach the stones. On breaking, each child would unclasp hands and comb the long green, mossy hair of an aged rock preparing it to greet the next group of children.

Downtown Vermilion, however, is little changed. Klaar's store for horse-collars, bridles, bits, and blankets has been supersede by a restaurant. Likewise George Becker's blacksmith shop where horses were shod and iceboat runners formed has been replaced with the Ritter Public Library. In contrast the Maudelton Hotel built by lumber dealer George and Mrs. Fischer and named after their two children, Maud and Elton, still silently stands kitty-corner from where it was, entertaining only its proud memories. In its dining room in 1911 Commodore and Mrs. Frederick W. Wakefield entertained Commodore and Mrs. Alexander Winton and others, from their visiting yacht *La Belle*. But total change has been small, possibly the result of the *Harbour Town 1837* concept, an effort at preserving the quaintness of the village and its many 19th century homes.

But it is in the number of pleasure craft calling Vermilion home that has most changed in seventy years. Americans are simply more affluent today. While these craft no longer have the 1877 Vermilion lighthouse of the west pier on which to head, they now have an exact duplicate on the grounds of the Inland Seas Maritime Museum.

Earlier we have spoken of the fish species taken from Lake Erie. Before closing a word should be said about Vermilion commercial fisheries in the 1920s, a period of large catches. Most fish landed at Vermilion docks at this time were caught in gill nets. A lesser, but substantial amount, however, were brought in by open trapnet boats, typically 35 to 40 feet in length, bearing only a small house covering the forward-placed gasoline engine. The men were always exposed. The gill net boats, in contrast, were steam-powered vessels 50 to 65 feet in length with a deck totally closed

Passenger vessels leave a trail of debris in their wake.
George P. Wakefield

The *Maudelton Hotel*, previously the *Lake House*, stood on the SE corner of Liberty and Main streets, circa. 1911.
The Vermilion Sesquicentennial Magazine.

A steam-powered fishing tug of the 1900-1940 era. George P. Wakefield

by housing. There was an opening at the stern from whence a cotton mesh net would be paid out by two men as the vessel steamed slowly forward. The nets would be in the lake one or two days depending on the temperature of the water. Fish spoil fast in summer temperature water. To port forward was an opening through which the nets, bearing entrapped fish, were taken from the water. From this steam-powered net-puller the net fell into a fish box with outward slanting sides. When one box was filled another box was substituted until all nets had been lifted from the water.

The nets lifted, the deckmen in oiled clothes would pull the net from the box across their laps, and with a small hook, placed in the eye of the fish, withdraw the creature from the mesh. With one movement the fish was snapped into boxes by species. The fish removed from the net, the net would then need be washed. Two men would accomplish this task. One paid out the net into the water from the stern of the vessel, the other man pulling in and coiling the rinsed net into a fish box as the vessel moved slowly toward home port.

On the starboard side of the vessel was an opening for taking on coal at the coal dock. The fuel was bunkered in the bilge area so as to be easily reached with a shovel by the engineer. The engineer acted as fireman as well. Forward on the starboard side was an opening which, when the boat was at the fish receiving dock the boxes of fish were unloaded. All openings could be closed in cold or inclement weather. On the rear deck was a steam pipe valve which allowed a bucket of lake water to be quickly heated with live steam. In this good samaritan bucket floated canvas gloves which could be slipped-on when handling the cold nets, then again reheated.

The net washing completed, the vessel would speed (about 10 miles per hour) to port. On arrival the vessel would first pull up to the coal dock. The vessel temporarily moored, the three deck men would push the coal car to the covered coal storage pile, load the car, then push it back to the vessel. There the coal would spill through a large deckport into the coal bunker. From the coal dock the vessel would then proceed to the fish dock.

The boat moored at the fish dock two deckmen would turn a loaded fish box upside down into a dock box. This latter box with vertical sides was equipped with two handles on each end for two men to carry and place on the weighing scale. The scale sat just inside the door of the fish house. In such a box would be about 300 pounds of fish all of one species. The fish weighed and their weight recorded, the fish would be dumped onto the wet floor of the fish house. There, house men would shovel the fish into a knocked-down box in which a shovel of crushed ice had been placed in the bottom. Possibly 200 pounds of fish would be shoveled in, another shovel of ice would be placed on top, and the lid nailed down. Such an operation would take no more than two minutes. The entire catch of boxed fish, all to one customer, would be carted by truck to a waiting railway express car, which the local steam train would pick up every day at 4:00 PM. Thus all hands knew when the perishable fish had to be at dockside.

With the fish transferred to the house men, the vessel would then proceed to the net drying area. The rinsed nets, carried ashore, would be wound by the deckmen on large wooden racks to dry.

A steam vessel carried five men. A captain, three deckmen, and an engineer. The engineer received a flat amount of money. The captain and each crew member would receive payment based on the value of the catch, to a mutually accepted formula. This payment schedule is true the world over, and was true on the *Pequod,* the whaler of *Moby Dick* on whom sailed raconteur Ishmael.

The 1940s saw the last of the steam vessel. George P. Wakefield, who knew these vessels thoroughly, illustrates one. Gasoline-powered gill-netters and trapnet fishing boats succeeded them. A trapnetter, powered by a gasoline-engine, carried only a crew of two. The fixed cost of a trapnetter was less than a gill net fishing boat. Also a liquid fuel is far easier and cleaner to load than coal. The later gillnetters carried a crew of four. No engineer. One is shown, the *Tessy II*, in Appendix C. To provide warm gloves for the fishermen, on the rear deck an elevated coal-stove with flat top bore a pail of water. On a trapnetter the pail of water was warmed from the engine manifold.

Ice for packing fish was cut in the winter. When the river ice was frozen to a thickness of 9 - 10 inches, cutting began. In early times one horse, properly shod so as not to slip, pulled a cutting blade which marked the ice to a depth of two inches. The horse was then directed to pull the blade at right angles across the former cutting. Thus were marked squares about thirty inches on a side. In subsequent years a machine did the marking. The fishermen, called back to work, bearing long saws with large teeth, would saw the ice lengthwise only. A segment of ice squares would be then directed by pike poles to the open water to an endless chain ice-lift. As the ice segment approached the lift a man with a sharpened, wide-blade crowbar-type instrument would strike the marked squares which would separate the ice into separate blocks. A block of ice weighed some 300 pounds. An endless chain belt constantly delivered ice blocks to the ice house.

Inside the ice house would be men who would erect the blocks onto their side, one nested against the other. With a first layer established, a layer of straw would be spread. The second layer would have the blocks horizontal. And so forth until the ice house was filled to the rafters. In ice cutting and storage possibly as many as 25 - 30 men, all regular fishermen, would be employed during the winter for typically three days.

In the fishing season a daily amount of ice blocks would be removed from the ice house, directed to an electrically-powered ice chipper, readying the ice for the incoming shipment of fish. Fresh water fisheries at that time throughout the world were not greatly different from the above. The author has visited a number of fisheries in the intervening years, and none were as efficiently run as these Vermilion fisheries.

In the 1930s the shipment of fish changed. Where before they were shovelled into boxes and shipped "in the round", the local fisheries began adding "value." The fish went from weighing scale to cutting tables. The scales were removed and the fillets sliced off. The rest of the fish was discarded. The fillies, ready for cooking, were shipped in tinned iced boxes. Such "value added" created some 20-30 more local jobs and, indeed, lowered shipping charges to the consumer.

Kishman Fish Company, Vermilion. Gasoline-powered gillnetters moored outside of trapnetters. L. to R.- fish house, ice house, cork house. To right would be: lead forge, coal house, net drying racks. All have disappeared. Art work courtesy Society Bank, Vermilion, Ohio, Artist Kinley Shogren, 1980.

ADDITIONAL READING

For additional general readings on lighthouses the literature is indeed rich. The book by Christine Moe, *Lighthouses and Lightships*, Monticello, Illinois: Vance Bibliographies, 1979 is worthwhile. Another: Douglas Bland Hague and Rosemary Christie, *Lighthouses: Their Architecture, History, and Archeology*, Llandysul: Gomer Press, 1975 is most interesting and would satisfy any architect of a lighthouse.

For early history on the 1877 Vermilion lighthouse Theodore Dunmore Wakefield learned from the U. S. National Archives the account which appears in the body of the text.

Appreciation for the letter written by the Office of Lighthouse Engineer in Oswego, New York to Professor Joseph Henry, L.L.D., Chairman, Lighthouse Board, Washington, D. C. concerning the 1877 Vermilion lighthouse is enhanced by reading the book by J. B. Crowther, *Famous American Men of Science*, New York: Norton, 1937. Another: Mary A. Henry, *Joseph Henry, Electrical Engineer*, *Scientific Monthly*, Sept. 1931. The life of Benjamin Franklin, who conceived of the lightning rod found on both the 1877 Vermilion lighthouse and its replica, may also be found in J. B. Crowther's book.

To learn more about vessel passage, such as the Lighthouse Tender *Haze,* through the Welland Canal of 1877 one may refer to the book by: Charles Hadfield. *The Canal Age*, New York, Frederick A. Praeger, 1968.

For reading about the Vermilion, Ohio replica 1877 lighthouse specifically, reference to the issues of *The Vermilion Photojournal*, 30 July 1991, and Vol. 32, No. 11, 29 October 1991 are of particular interest.

For learning how whale oil was secured for lamps Herman Melville's *Moby Dick* is, of course, the classic source. Then the finding of petroleum by Colonel Edward Lauretine Drake, an act which led to the displacement of whale-oil by kerosene as a fuel for light sources, is helpful. While no book appears to exist on Drake, a good encyclopedia such as the *Americana* records he was the first to drill for oil, discovering it in Titusville, Pennsylvania 27 August 1869. From his first well he obtained 25 barrels a day at a depth of 60 feet. It was the initiation of large scale production.

Drake's discovery and the almost simultaneous development of the kerosene lantern resulted in the Civil War Union forces, for the first time in warfare, reading maps on the battlefield by light from a lantern rather than from a candle. Indeed, at Gettysburg, on the night of the Third Day - after the abortive attack on Union forces by Maj. Gen. George Edward Pickett, "Pickett's Charge" - General Robert E. Lee discussed the Confederate retreat by candlelight with Brig. Gen. John D. Imboden, the Confederate forces being *sans* lanterns. Troops under Imboden would escort the 17-mile long train of Confederate wounded and supplies from Gettysburg to Winchester, Virginia.

Regardless of the light source used for lighthouses Augustin Jean Fresnel development of the lens bearing his name was seminal. For more information on Fresnel and his experiments Henry Crew, *The Wave Theory of Light: Memoirs of Huygens,* Young, and *Fresnel*, New York:

American Book Co., 1900, is one of the rare sources of interest. Also of value is the text used by the author when studying optics: Charles F. Meyers. *The Diffraction of Light, X-Rays, and Material Particles,* 1934, and Archie Frederick Collins, *Experimental Optics*, 1933. After Fresnel's death the French government issued *Oeuvres Complètes d'Augustin Fresnel* (1866-1870). Because of the book's complex organization his experiments and development of theory are difficult to follow.

For readings on early electric light sources *Thomas Edison's 1879 Incandescent Lamp, Scientific American* Vol. LXLII No. 2 10 Jan. 1880, p. 19. is pivotal. For later electric light sources writing the General Electric Lamp Division, Nela Park, Cleveland will be found helpful. The author tested inumerable light sources in their Photometric Laboratory as a young scientist in 1937.

For the genesis of the generation of electric power the recent book by John Meurig Thomas, *Michael Faraday and the Royal Institution: The Genius of Man and Place*, New York: Am. Inst. of Physics, 1991 is most revealing. Then to illustrate how mid-19th century scientists approached generating electricity the reference *Early Electric Generators*, *Scientific American,* Vol. XXIV, No. 3557, 4 November 1882, pp. 5695-6 is most helpful. Many variations on generators were made in passing from Hipolyte Pixii's ring machine generator to more modern means. For creating electric power today reading the journal *Power Plant Engineering* can be rewarding.

Finally, in understanding photocells, the present device for turning on-and-off the light source in modern lighthouses *The Solarex Guide to*

Solar Electricity, 1983, edited by Edward Robertson and by the Technical Staff of Solarex Corporation will be found most helpful.

Probably the richest treasure trove of writings on Vermilion maritime activities, both early and present, is owned by George Patterson Wakefield. “I have a trunk full,” he has told the author. A large portion of it has been published in a weekly marine column George writes for the Vermilion *Photojournal*, but surely much probably has not seen the light of day. George has masterful knowledge of the Great Lakes and the vessels which sail on them.

Schr. *Vermillion*, Solomon Parsons, Builder, 1814, 36.89 tons.
George P. Wakefield.

APPENDIX A

A SESQUICENTENNIAL HISTORY OF VERMILION
The French Period
1669-1762

Theodore Dunmore Wakefield

French names abound from Vermilion westward: La Chapelle Creek, Huron River, Portage River, La Carne, La Carpe Creek, La Toussaint River, etc. Vermilion itself is of French derivation - *Vermilion*, meaning red, of course. Yet very little is known about French exploration along the south shore of Lake Erie.

Sanson's map of 1656 names and outlines the lake with reasonable accuracy, no doubt from Indian descriptions. It wasn't actually 'discovered" until 1669 when Adrien Jolliet traversed the north shore west to east. That year two missionaries met Jolliet who told them of his passage on the lake. They recorded their visit to Lake Erie at Grand River near Long Point, where they spent the winter.

On March 23, 1670, they erected a cross and took possession of our area in the name of the King of France.

> "We, the undersigned, certify that we have seen erected on the lands of the lake named Erie the arms of the King of France at the foot of a cross, with this inscription:
>
> In the year of salvation, 1669, Clement IX being seated on the throne of St. Peter, Louis XIV reigning in France, and Monsieur Talon being deputy of the King, having arrived in this place two missionaries of the Seminary of Montreal, accompanied by seven other French, who are the first of all Europeans to have wintered on this

A Sesquicentennial History of Vermilion

Theodore D. Wakefield

The French Period
1669-1762

Lakes Superior, Huron, Michigan, Erie, and Ontario were French.
Inland Seas Maritime Museum

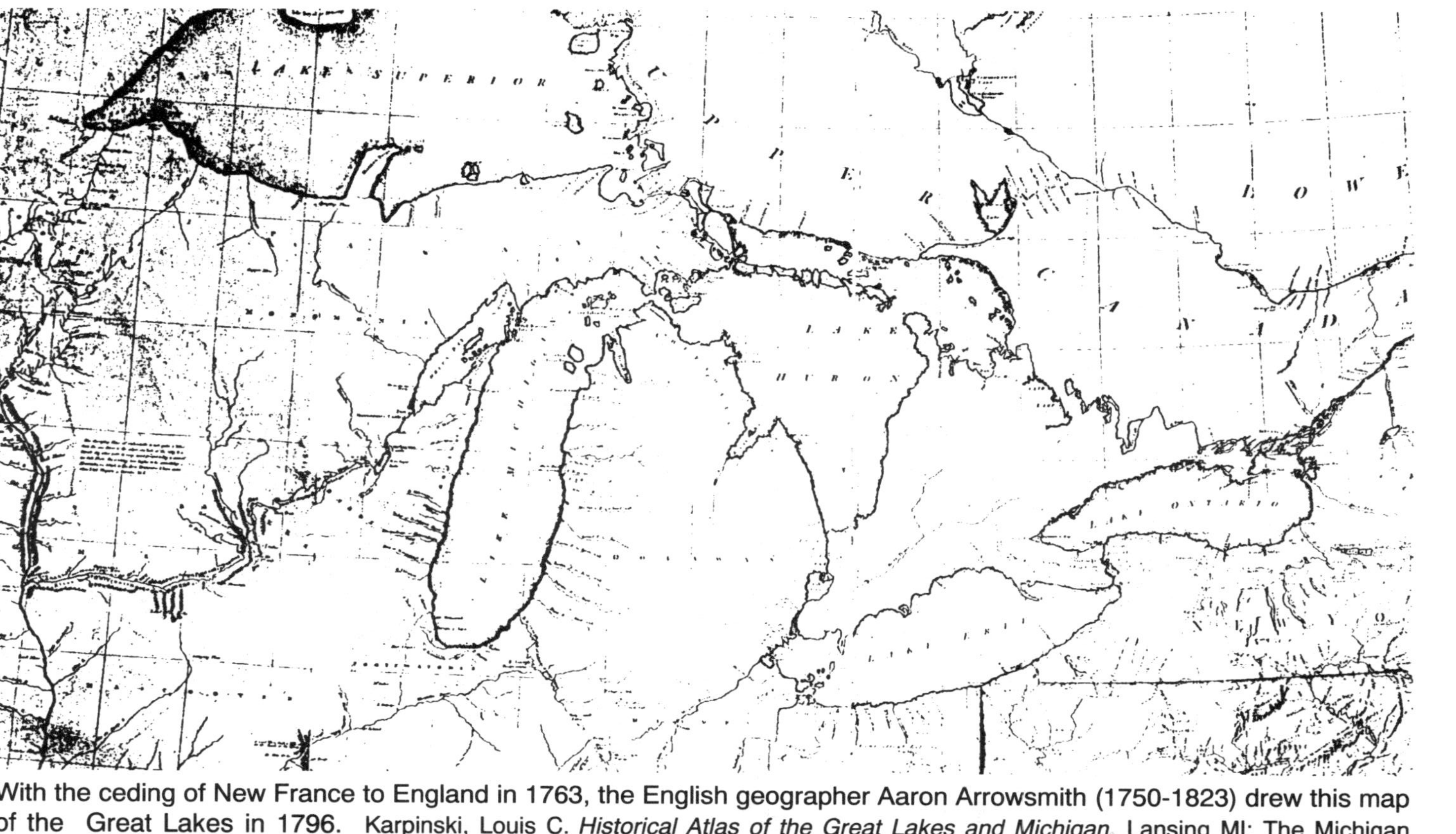

With the ceding of New France to England in 1763, the English geographer Aaron Arrowsmith (1750-1823) drew this map of the Great Lakes in 1796. Karpinski, Louis C. *Historical Atlas of the Great Lakes and Michigan*, Lansing MI: The Michigan Historical Commission, 1931, p. 77.

lake, of which they have taken possession in the name of their King, as a non-occupied land, by the placing of his Coat of Arms, which they have attached at the foot this cross. In faith, we have signed the present certificate. Signed: Francois Dolier, priest of the diocese of Nantes, in Brittany, De Galiné, deacon of the diocese of Rennes, in Brittany."

Later, at the time of discussions between France and England in 1687, the French government sent the above transcript and Galiné's map to London as incontestable proof of France's rights to Lake Erie, Ontario, and the surrounding territory.

On the 26th of March, the explorers launched their canoes and paddled toward the west, hugging the north shore and camping each night on the beach. After 250 kilometers of paddling they reached the mouth of the Detroit River. Galiné honestly reported: "*Je ne marque que ce que j'ai vu.* I note only what I've seen." He saw Point Pelee and the northernmost of the islands in western Lake Erie.

Dolier and Galiné and many who followed later, purposely avoided the south shore because it was controlled by the Iroquois (Indians) who had killed or driven out the Erie Indians in 1655 and who were mortal enemies of the French. Even as late as 1755, Bellin, engineer of the King for the French navy and drafter of an excellent map of the Great Lakes, inscribed the south shore of Lake Erie with the phrase, "*Toute cette coste n'est presque pas connue*. All this shore is almost unknown."

With the fall of Quebec in 1759 and ceding of New France to England in 1763, Lake Erie and Vermilion came under the rule of the King of England.

Thus ended the French period with little or no written history of our area.

Except for the ever remindful place names, probably given by *coureurs du bois* and *voyageurs*, not noted for their education or for recording their travels with maps or by the written word, we would never know that we are in former French jurisdiction, (a period) which lasted over 90 years.

French *Fleur de Lis*

APPENDIX B

VERMILION'S LAST AMERICAN INDIAN

Ernest Henry Wakefield

Fred Platte was the last remaining American Indian in Vermilion. He was a Menomonee. I knew him well in the 1920s and early 30s when he was perhaps 50-60 years old. While not in the physical prime of life I have seen him scramble-up the spar of a sloop using the sail-hoist only as an aid.

Fred never, to my knowledge, had a squaw and, I believe, left no scion. He lived on the lakeshore in the basement of the former Gidding's home, and for daily watering used the facilities of the nearby Vermilion water pumping station.

Fred always bore a well-tanned face and body. He had a deeply furrowed face, sparse auburn hair, a prominent nose, and visible veins on his auburn hirsute arms. On his left bicep, where little hair grew, he had an anchor tattoed. He dressed winter and summer in self-made, unhemmed, 10-ounce canvas trousers, a blue cotton shirt open at the neck, white tennis shoes *sans* socks. He protected himself from the cold with a dark-blue pea jacket. In summer he seemed not to sweat even when completing tasks in the hottest sun.

Fred earned a modest living, and his wants were small, primarily by being a professional sailor and handy man around the increasing number of yachts which began peppering the Vermilion river in the late 20s and early 30s. In a period of great corruption due to the investure of rum-running into the Vermilion river, tales told by George P. Wakefield and Karen Cornelius in Appendices C and D, Fred was scrupulously honest and had nothing to do with this illegal lake and river-borne trade. Nor did I ever see him drink, or use tobacco.

Fred was most helpful in furthering my knowledge of boats and of yachting. I cite two examples. With brother George at the tiller, a sloop in my care suffered a broken mast principally from dry rot. Because a wooden spar need be made from strait-grained and flexible wood, spruce was chosen. Since the replacement spar required a 34-foot timber I ordered a knot-free 6 x 6 inch piece from a Cleveland lumber company through the local Fischer Lumber Company, a request which could only be filled in the American northwest. This element arrived in Vermilion by railroad and special motor-truck. Fred showed me how to adze the wood to roughly the correct tapered size. Final shaping was by a steel plane. Then sandpapering, and finally varnishing.

At another time Fred was helping me apply deck canvas on a sloop. Resting for a moment, he sat back on his haunches and volunteered, "Ernie, the first rule for safety in sailing is to keep the water on the *outside* of the boat." Then he laughed, not aloud as I did, but as an Indian, by placing his right index finger beside his ample nose, his chiseled face meanwhile showing deeper creases of delight.

While maturing I listened to him tell stories surely more than one-hundred times while he sat on an overturned, well-worn fish-box in George Goetz's twine-house.

For completeness in listing the three rules of safety on the water I add the two others related by my father, Commodore Frederick William Wakefield. Rule 2:- "If caught on the lake with a squall approaching, when to windward you see wind on the water (for it darkens the surface) take your canvas (sail) down and run with the wind, for you never know how hard it will blow." Rule 3:- "In an accident at sea, *always* stay with the boat."

Failure to practice Rule 1 led to a drowning of a teen-ager, off-shore, just north of the Inland Seas Marine Museum. Failure to practice Rule 2 caused the well-seasoned sailor, brother Albert F. Wakefield, to lose a spar just west of the 1877 Vermilion lighthouse. And failure to heed Rule 3 caused the death of an only child near Put-in-Bay, the death of an older couple east of the 1877 Vermilion lighthouse, and an airline hostess off-shore before Northwestern University, Evanston, Illinois. In all cases I was a contemporary and not far removed.

Fred Platte to me was a friend, a mentor, and a helper. When I left for the university my life entered a new phase. When, after four years, I returned he had joined his ancestors. Life along the *River,* always interesting, had changed.

APPENDIX C

APPLEBY OF CHICKENNOLEE, OR STEER FOR THE VERMILION LIGHTHOUSE

CAPTAIN JACK (George Patterson Wakefield)

In this account it is necessary to realize Chickenolee Reef is in Canadian waters as seen in the accompanying map. The United States, at the time, prohibited the use or transport of alcoholic liquors. Editor.

Chickennolee is a little known rocky reef lying eastward of the southern portion of Pelee Island in Lake Erie. Presumably, it's name was derived from the Hen and Chicken Islands lying on the west side of Pelee in this manner: In the 18th century when the reef was a small rocky mass jutting above the water some early explorer noted the island was another Chicken Island, in relation to Pelee. It was, however, out of the normal lee of easterly winds, hence *Chicken-no-lee* became its name. The name stuck.

Clint Appleby is less known to modern yachtsmen than Chickennolee Reef, but in the 1920s Clint was the "King of the Rock" to Lake Erie boatmen from Amherstburg, Ontario to Erie, Pennsylvania. In those grand old days liquor was a lake commodity which attracted adventurous lake fisherman from their legitimate trade. Our Appleby was one of those characters. In fact, he may have been one of the most unforgettable bootleggers of our time.

Appleby's usual run was between Kingsville, Ontario and some port between Toledo and Cleveland, depending mainly upon the circumstances along shore such as: 1) local facilities, 2) frequency of previous landings, and 3) the presence of Federal patrols. Generally his policy was one of great secrecy of destination coupled with the confusion of infrequency.

Clint would load a cargo at Kingsville and make for Chickennolee where he would spend his time at random thereby upsetting his time of arrival in the States as determined from his departure from Canada. It was impossible to leave Kingsville with a "load" and not be reported to Federal forces who signaled the "Rummie" patrol who would then take to sea with their 75-foot Coast Guard cutters.

This whole procedure forced Appleby to spend much time around Chickennolee Reef. Consequently, he quite naturally became a sport fisherman. Fortunately for Clint Chickennolee was the finest fishing grounds on Lake Erie. This diversion was much safer than "tasting the cargo," let us say. Clint was very strict about this sort of thing. For instance, when he had a liquid load aboard the *Tessy II* no one was allowed a taste. Conversely, when the good ship was free of contraband Appleby was another person. It was easy to tell whether he was coming or going by the cut of her prow for then the *Tessy II* was indeed a happy ship.

The *Tessy II* was a fast gillnetter Clint built in Vermilion for the fishing trade. She was of the light displacement type that Ed Lampe had originated in the twenties - cypress strip-planked with a sharp bow and a wide, flat stern. Since Clint powered her with two 150-horsepower Kermath engines many a fishermen blinked his eyes at all the extra power for gillnetting, but most of them knew the real purpose for all the "steam" – to outspeed the Federal cutters.

The *Tessy II* was housed from stem to stern and appeared to be a conventional gillnetter except for one detail below decks. Here she had permanent bulkheads for'd and aft of the engine room. Each compartment was accessible by a hatch. The one forward just abaft the for'd a bit, and the after one a flush manhole. The latter provided access to the rudder-post stuffing-box, but the quadrant and the rudder-post prevented easy entry. There was barely enough room to reach in with a long arm for tightening the gland. This inconvenience or poor design didn't bother Clint.

Seldom does a commercial fisherman take up sport fishing. It is almost a sacrilege. In all my years observing fishermen of both varieties in Vermilion port, which was both a leading sport and commercial fishing center of the Great Lakes, I had never met a hybrid type - a *netter* turned *hooker* or a hooker turned netter.

This peculiar shift of Clint's was enough to convince any jury that he was a rum-runner, but such evidence was never needed as Clint had never been apprehended.

The *Tessy II* headed out of Kingsville harbor one morning with a rich load of two-hundred cases of H & H destined for the usual port, the west dock of Pelee Island. The *Tessy II* was legally merely a freight boat ferrying a load to the Canadian island of Pelee. In those days the island was consigned sufficient liquor and beer to sink the place, but the authorities were indoctrinated thoroughly to the profession so as not to overload the island. A local boat could take all the tea in China as long as she went to China. To say the custom authorities were cooperative would

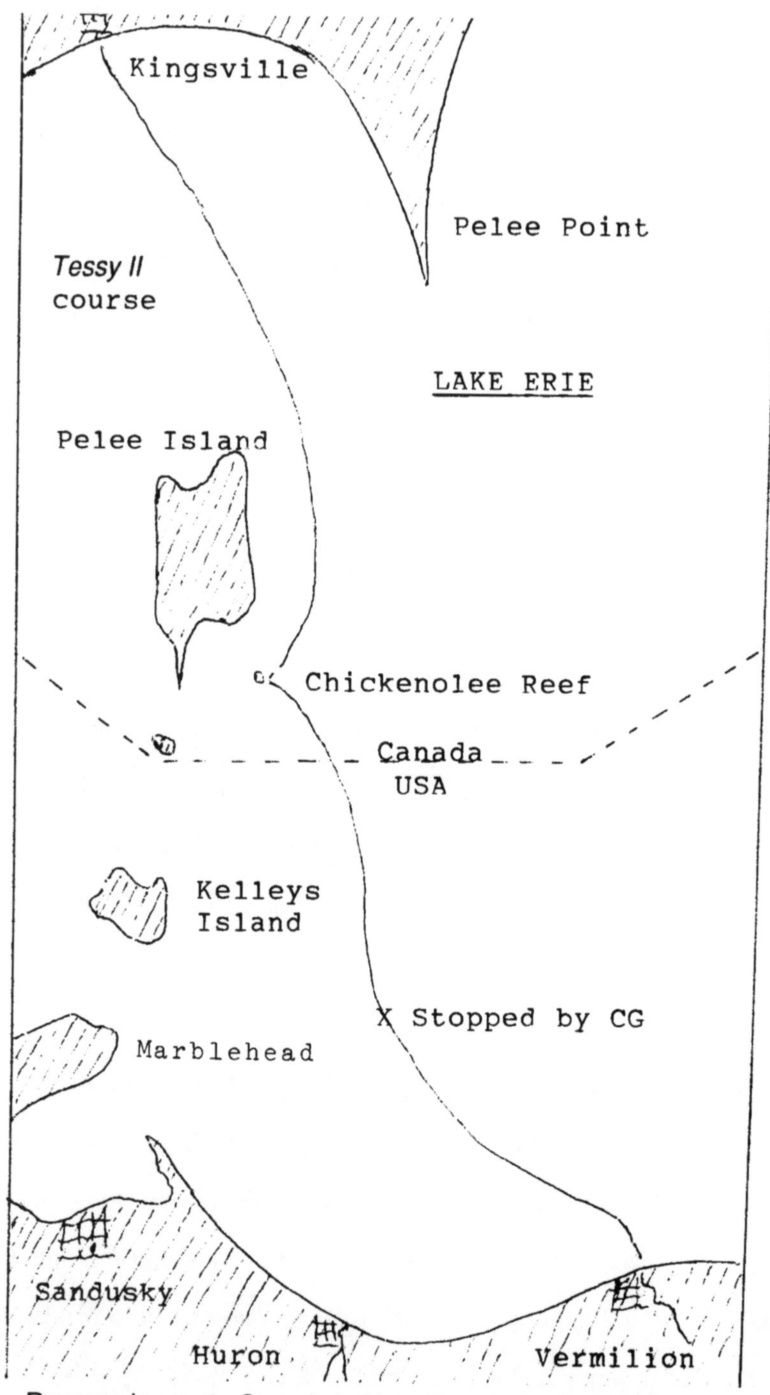

Rumrunning route Canada to Vermilion during Prohibition.
George P. Wakefield

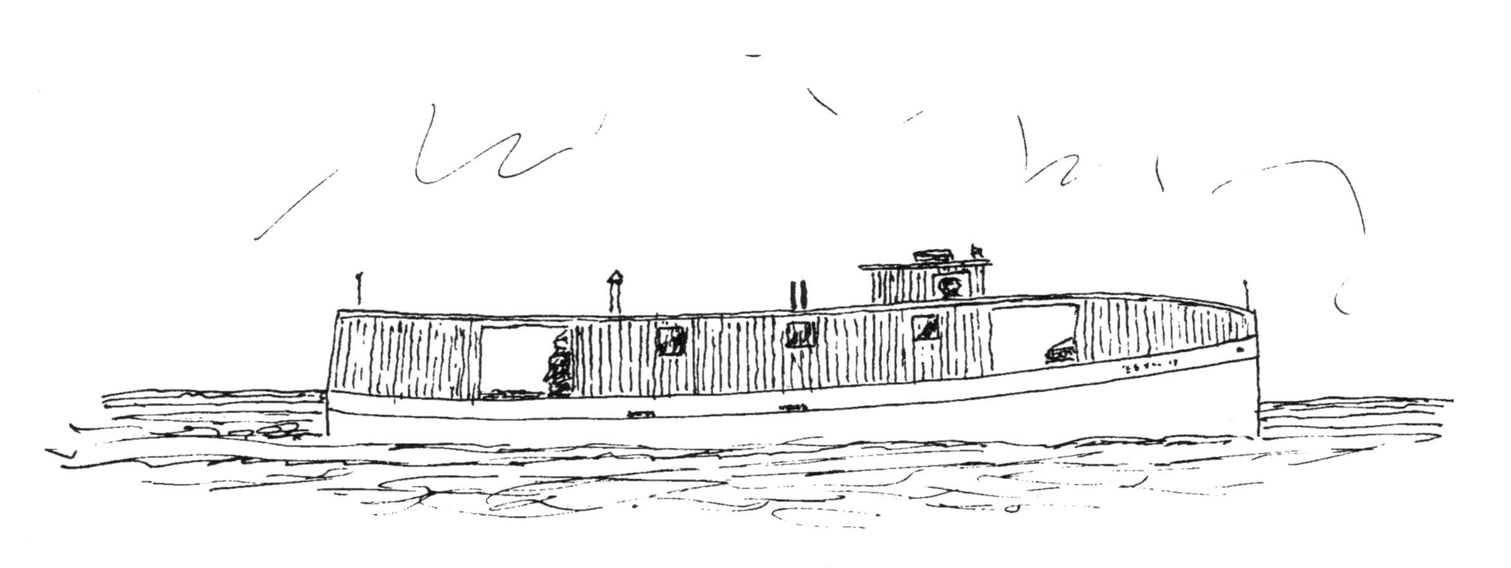

Rumrunner *Tessy II* was a housed, high-speed fish boat. George P. Wakefield

be slanderous. They were operating strictly according to the law. So was Clint; he even had a Canadian non-resident sport-fishing license!

Clint set his course for the coast of Pelee and his favorite fishing spot. A breeze from the southwest kicked-up a small chop which rolled the *Tessy II* on her way. If it blew harder Chickennolee would be a nice lee for the night. If the wind shifted to the east Clint could easily round the southern end and lay in the lee of Fish Point. With basic provisions and a stove aboard Clint could remain at sea for as long as a week.

On this trip Clint figured a three day lapse would confuse the patrols sufficiently to clear the way for a beach-landing east of Vermilion. He had to elude the CG 219 (Coast Guard cutter 219) for sure. It was the cutter stationed at Vermilion port.

At the reef Clint was in perfectly flat water. What a day to fish! He stopped the T*essy II* and drift-fished with his line over the stern. The only missing item was a tall glass of H & H and tinkling ice. Clint was an ardent fisherman. He would just as soon fish for three days as run for a port. In the past he had caught some fine black bass and blue pike on the reef. He had also hooked onto a couple of big ones that he couldn't land. Consequently, Clint fished with heavy tackle as if he were really out for the record. The fish were there and he had plenty of time.

Clint's crew, his only one, was a fisherman by the name of Slim Ranney. Slim had fished and drifted all his life and was sort of a Lake Erie bum. Little did it matter to Slim if he fished or "rummied" as long as he could take his afternoon nap in a twine box on a gill netter. It was Slim's ideal spot for napping or sobering. Slim was snoozing as usual when he was suddenly awakened by an abnormal shipboard noise.

"I've got him, I've got him, Slim, he's that big one. I'm going to get him this time." The fish was running wide and Clint was checking his reel with a gloved hand the best he could. At the end of the run Clint was busy bringing in the slack, hand over hand. By now, Slim had secured the gaff-hook ready for the critical landing, but he was premature for Clint had a lot of fighting to do before he could get the fish near the boat.

"This fish is a whopper and full of steam. It's going to be a long battle, Slim."

"Can I help, Clint?" Now, excited by the chase, Slim had suddenly become a sport fisherman. He had risen to the task like a true fisherman as he stood near Clint with gaff in hand.

Clint braked and pulled for a whole hour before they caught sight of the monster.

"It's a shark, Slim, my God! I never saw a fish like this before! Get ready with the gaff, Slim."

Clint gradually managed to bring the fish in and Slim gave him the hook and lifted with all his might.

"It's a sturgeon, Slim, and a big one. Good god, he must be eight-feet long. We'll never get him aboard with that gaff."

Clint picked up a line and secured it to the shank of the gaff- hook.

By pulling hard the fish came above the water about a foot and a half. This was sufficient for Clint to put a net-box hook into each gill of the monster. He soon had a tackle secured to a roof carline and the box hooks, and was pulling hard when the strain on the bulwarks tore away the bolt fitting and the whole fish came sliding aboard like a rocket. The fish hit Slim and sent him sprawling to the deck. Clint fell into an empty fish box as the unexpected release caught him off balance.

"Cripes, what a fish!" piped Slim as he recovered from the body blow.

"My god, isn't he something! This is the biggest fish I have ever seen. He must be eight-feet long and over four-hundred pounds."

Clint went forward and came back with a carpenter's rule. He opened it to six-feet and laid it on the fish with one end at the tip of the tail.

"Six-feet," and he shifted the ruler even with the fish's nose as he turned over the rule to read the inches.

"Twenty-nine inches more. That's eight-feet, five-inches. Slim, how's that for a catch?"

"Couldn't have been any bigger. As it is, he damn near wrecked the boat coming aboard the way he did. If he had been any larger he might have crashed right through the cabin into the engine room."

"Yeah, he'd perhaps knocked our engines out, too. Guess we were lucky."

By now the reality of such a whale aboard caused Clint to ponder his original goal of unloading his Scotch east of Vermilion. The fish had altered his plans because it was a large one. He certainly wouldn't be able to lay off Pelee for three days, and he didn't want to take the fish to Pelee. He had his pride. He had to go to Vermilion to show the boys the size fish we catch on Chickennolee, reasoned Clint. He was now anxious to get going. He would leave Chickennolee at nightfall and take the chance with the Feds.

As the sun set in the west over the Bass Islands the *Tessy II* was on course to Vermilion. It was dark when she crossed the imaginary international border between Canada and the United States. Another two hours and Vermilion would show her weak red light marking the west pierhead.

The *Tessy II* was perking along in fine style when suddenly the port engine started missing.

"Take the wheel, Slim. I'll go below and see what's the trouble."

Clint crawled down beside the wavering Kermath engine and tried some checks in order to diagnose the ailment. It was the lack of gas or water in the fuel. He climbed back to the pilot house and turned the key on the port engine.

"I'll have to clean the line or filter. You hold her on course. Maybe I can get her going soon."

With that Clint went back to his cripple and started to work.

He got the line apart at the carburetor and was just about to place his mouth on the gas line and blow back into the gas tank when the starboard engine slowed down.

"It's the Coast Guard, Clint!" shouted Slim.

Now he could hear the siren. He regained the pilot house and killed the remaining engine for silence. Now the siren was abeam and the seventy-five footer loomed to port.

"Get ready for boarding," shouted a hand on the Coast Guard.

Soon three Coast Guard sailors scrambled aboard through the

for'd doorway. They each brandished 45's and bore flashlights.

"This is a search , Captain. What have you got aboard?"

"Nothing but fish, Bos'n," answered Clint.

"Are you kiddin' Captain. We'll take a look." With that they all went aft.

"Crying out loud, look at this fish!"

"Man oh man, you guys aren't loaded with fish, you're loaded with *a fish*!"

The boarding party was amazed. They caught the spirit of the catch. The Bos'n sent one sailor for'd and another one to the engine room. He took his flashlight and aimed it into the after hatch and saw nothing but the obstructing rudder-quadrant. He put the cover back in place.

"How did you fellows get this whale?"

Clint told him the story as the other two sailors came back and listened. The big fish and story completely baffled the boarding party. They were convinced that Clint was a bonafide fisherman. The bos'n went forward and waved his light. The cutter came along side again. As the sailors left, the Bos'n called to Clint, "Okay, Captain, carry on with the fish."

Clint stood at the doorway as the cutter started ahead. He heard something about "a whale of a fish" before the roar of the cutter's twin Sterling engines passed by in the darkness.

Clint made his landfall and delivered his Scotch. The next morning the *Tessy II* unloaded the fish at Kishman's dock. Many townspeople came to see the unusual catch. A photographer from the *Vermilion News* wanted a picture of Clint with his fish.

"Where's Clint?" asked the cameraman.

Phil Darley, the fish house foreman who stood guard over the sturgeon, replied, “He’s down on the *Tessy* fixing the rudder. The damn quadrant came off last night and he’s putting it back. I guess he hit a rock on Chickennolee.”

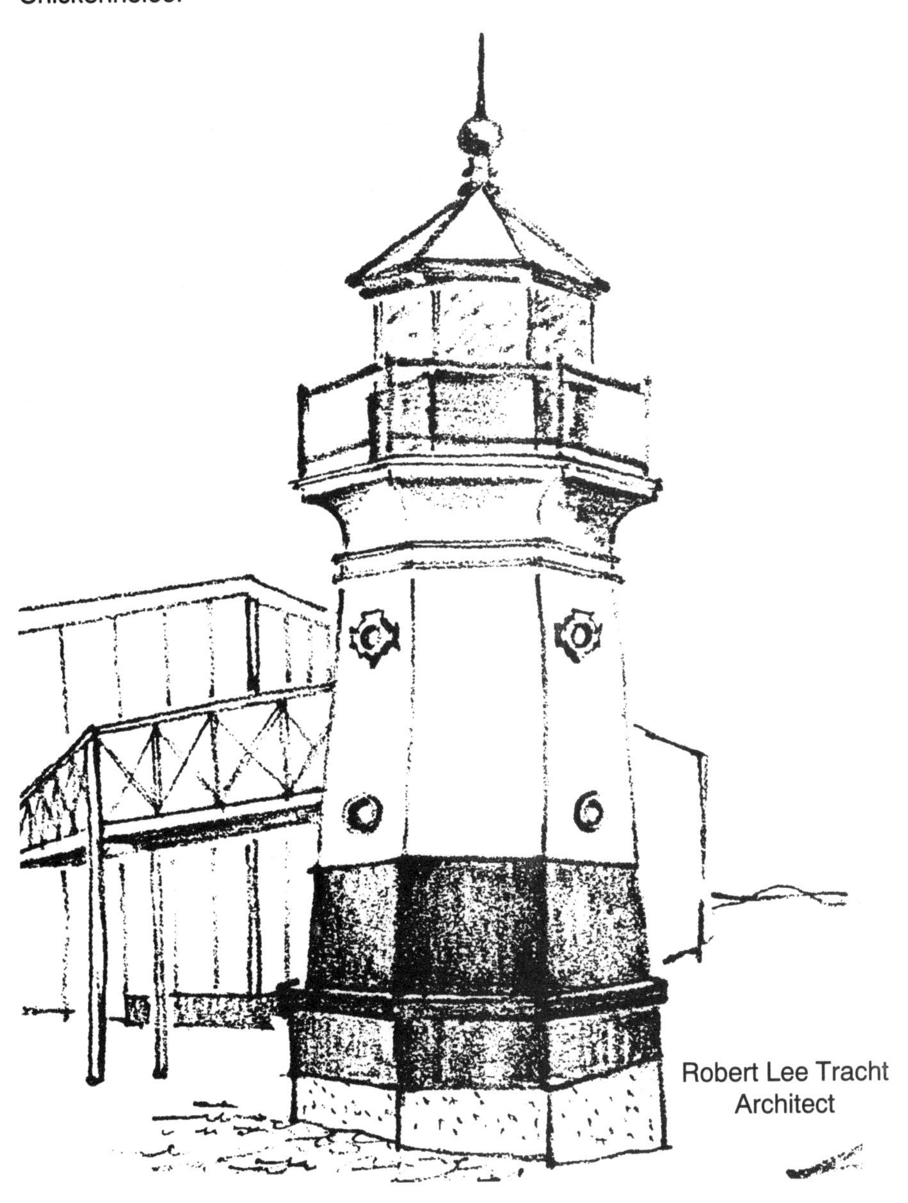

APPENDIX D

PROHIBITION DAYS WERE OFT WET AND WILD

Karen Cornelius

With the dawn of Prohibition in 1920, Vermilion's history took on a wild, adventurous edge. Local citizens of the day, a stable population of 1,500 watched their small harbor become infamous as a prime drop-off point for illegal beer, ale, and liquor from Canada.

By 1925, the village found itself in the midst of the Lake Erie whiskey war between federal agents and the U. S. Coast Guard on one hand chasing the daredevil rumrunners and crafty bootleggers on the other. As town folks went their merry way, Prohibition patrols doggedly watched the waterways and even set up roadblocks once in a while to capture those scamps who drove trucks loaded with the demon spirits to larger cities.

Heresay from several of Vermilion's present-day senior citizens seem to confirm the fact that the "bad guys" received more support from the residents then the law enforcement officials. Needless to say, the 13-year dry spell mandated by the Constitution's 18th amendment was a failure ending in a 1933 repeal.

On a national scale, Prohibition spawned more crime, not less. Smuggling, graft, and violence built a large, flourishing illegitimate liquor industry across the United States. Although Chicago had its Al Capone and New York City it "Legs" Diamond, Vermilion participants never made the big leagues nor even came close to the hard-core crime and gangland shootouts.

"There was a lot of bootlegging going on, but there was no violence," recalled a long-time resident and former mayor Fred Fischer of Washington Street. "There were more funny incidents than anything," he said. "You have to remember Vermilion was only a small town then with one night watchman, and he had one glass eye," stated Fischer. "There was not a police department."

"It didn't seem that dishonorable or criminal at the time," said Huron Street resident Ted Wakefield. "It got to be so ridiculous after a while they repealed Prohibition and made liquor legal again," he said. Wakefield, who was just a boy at the time, agreed Vermilion had no one the likes of Al Capone, but said he had heard many of the town's most prominent citizens were involved at the time.

Main Street resident Al Buell concurred that many of the people who sold, stored, and transported the liquor were the town's most staid citizens. "It was lucrative, and no one thought it was a terrible thing to do." said Buell.

When Grand Street resident Alvin Snell came to Vermilion around 1920, he was considered an outsider so it was hard for him to tell how much money was actually being made during Prohibition. "I knew it was going on, but wasn't involved." Many people, he pointed out, harmlessly made their own small supplies so they could have something to take to the dances. "I made dandelion wine," he said.

Snell, who still remembers the great chicken dinners and room and board at the former Wagner Hotel for $12 per week, said there was often night-time activity along the Main Street beach. He related how flashing lights in the dark were meant to signal boats filled with contraband it was safe to come into shore.

Fischer, Wakefield, and Buell all tell of the 75-foot Coast Guard cutters stationed near the present waterworks for several years during Prohibition. "We'd go swimming and see them there daily," said Fischer.

Buell quipped it was heard that some guardsmen were not that serious about their duties and would make a run into the lake to intercepts some liquor when their own stock ran out. Wakefield said the government boats didn't seem to deter the rumrunners who often would be unloading less than two blocks away from the moored Coast Guard.

If the rumrunner were pursued in hot chase across the lake, they would dump their wares overboard to lighten the boats for a quicker escape. The illegal spirits, of course, would eventually float to shore and that's when the average Vermilionite got a chance to enjoy the profits of Prohibition for free.

Wakefield stated the bottles would wash up on the beach in burlap sacks. "As boys, we'd pick up the sacks and store them," he said. "That was how I got my first taste of beer," laughed Wakefield.

"One day we found seven sacks frozen in the sand," related Buell who was one of those young boys. He said each sack had 24 bottles of ale and the teenagers quickly took the booty to their clubhouse as private stock. "It was supposed to be a secret, but the next day half the people in town were down on the (Main Street) beach with rakes and shovels," chuckled Buell.

The men stated that actually the kids didn't drink that much.

"We wouldn't dare come home with alcohol on our breath. We'd be in big trouble." said Buell. Once the clubhouse bunch made their own brew which wasn't quite right. They had more fun punching nails in the bottle caps and chasing each other with the pressurized liquid spurting every which way.

Many more collected stories suggest large quantities of beer and liquor were brought into the country through such lakeside communities as Port Clinton, Sandusky, Huron, Vermilion, and Lorain. The sources were most often key Ontario locations such as Kingsville, Leamington, and Pelee Island. "Vermilion couldn't possibly consume all of it," said Wakefield who thought a lot went into Cleveland.

Serious rumrunning was done with high-power speedboats. Although it was suspected some fishing tugs may have been used to carry liquor loads in their netting, none of the local commercial fishing companies actually did any of the rumrunning. The ice houses conveniently on the river's edge may, however, have been great storage bins for booze as were the farmers' barns.

Mr. Buell heard tell of an amusing escapade regarding a Jefferson Street duplex where an attic was used for storage. As the story goes, a local resident found some whiskey in an ice house under the straw, and he decided to take it home by truck. He unloaded the cargo in his neighbor's attic because his side of the duplex had been raided before.

The neighbor discovered the liquor, and invited the original thief to a ballgame one night. In the meantime, the neighbor arranged for a friend to come in and haul the whiskey out of the attic so they could have it to themselves. Unfortunately the friend and the liquor disappeared, and both duplex residents were foiled by yet the third thief on the scene.

Another tale remembered by many and validated by the local *Vermilion News* published in October 1925 was about a rumrunning boat from Canada called the *Zarkin* which beached west of town off Rumsey Park. The crew threw several hundred cases of beer and ale overboard then abandoned ship never to be found again.

The local newspaper reported "cold, wet-footed citizens on shore quenched their thirst with real beer, real foam cooled by the chilling Lake Erie waves." The boat itself was sold by the U. S. Collector of Customs for $800 to a Vermilion resident who repaired and commissioned it for the sand trade.

The 62-year-old newspaper account also mentioned the fact that more mischief was going on about the town concerning "those ships that come in the night." The paper stated a "well-known law enforcer of the county watched the *bulldog* at one end of the river while at the other, a small boat unloaded into a truck and drove away before Vermilionites paid much attention."

The mayor at the time, Harry R. Williams, was quoted as saying, "This disgrace must be stopped." The *Vermilion News* commented as far as the village was concerned, they were not so sure it was a disgrace.

Rumrunner patrol

For example: in 1928, a familiar sight was a patrol boat like this one, the Coast Guard 219, looking for bootlegging rum runners. Vermilion Photojournal 20 July 1987, Karen Cornelius.

APPENDIX E

GOLD, A WATERSPOUT, AND THE LIGHTHOUSE

Ernest Henry Wakefield

Since the beginning of time gold, because of unchanging quality over time and its scarcity, has stirred the hearts of men and sent them on quests. While I have cruised the Fraser River where it swirls down from the Coast Mountains in extreme southwestern Canada, and have followed the Snake river as it winds through the Tetons, and have hunted the outcropping where the Grand Canyon etches through the Colorado Plateau, it was the Vermilion river and its environs which led to gold.

I observed gold near Vermilion in a singular way. But let me relate how this good fortune occurred, and how fate intervened to keep the gold, perhaps ever after, in Vermilion, out of reach of any present day Tantalus.[1]

Those yachtsmen and fellow town's people over seventy years of age will remember the old Vermilion lighthouse, a picture of which is on the cover. This light, before the local age of electricity, had as the its source a kerosene-fired beacon. Captain J. H. Burns, the then local lightkeeper, walked the pier each evening, fair weather and foul, and hung the lantern inside the Fresnel lens to alert passing or incoming vessels.

---

1. *Greek mythology.* "A wealthy king, son of Zeus and father of Pelops and Niobe. For an atrocious sin (cannibalism) Tantalus was punished in the lower world by being placed on the midst of a lake whose water reached his chin, but receded whenever he attempted to allay his thirst, while over his head hung branches laden with choice fruit which likewise receded when ever he stretched out his hand to grasp them." Derivative: To tantalize.

Captain Burns lived on the southwest corner of Liberty and Grand street in a house owned by the federal government, as identified in Appendix F. Each evening he placed his lamp. Twice weekly he washed the windows around the prism. Between prism and sash a man could easily walk. On sickness of Burns, a local boy would be engaged to hang the lamp. Usually it was my brother, Albert F. Wakefield, who as a boy would do this chore on the indisposition of Burns. By the time I came along the Vermilion lighthouse was electrified and a blinking white light - one second on, seven seconds off. Subsequently the Vermilion light burned a steady red, appropriately for the village name.

My father, Commodore Frederick William Wakefield, was the local weatherman. We boys, naturally, became more than normally conscious of the weather. All of us, Ted, George, Fred, Bill, Albert and yes, Ruth, took turns in hoisting the weather flags at the old homestead, now the genesis structure of the Inland Seas Maritime Museum. Occasionally, I would accompany Burns out to the light when window washing was to be done. And it was on one of these visits that I observed the presence of gold!

AN ONRUSHING WATERSPOUT

Burns and I were washing the inside of the lantern windows. Burns would scour the top, which was was out my reach, while I would polish the bottom. Engaged in this operation on a hot summer afternoon as we were, Burns glanced to the west, off Sherod's Reef, and there observed a squall making-up. A black one. Soon the low flying scud passed overhead. The flat water riffled and frightened. Early puffs chiseled the placid surface. A spider, his web outside between the over hang and the glass, scampered up his net to a safer recess. The old sloop *Fredricka,* her sails taut, slipped in with Fred Platte at the tiller. George Krapp, who had been fishing for catfish, up-ended his bamboo, threw the extra angleworms into the river, and idled into safety. "Cloudy" Noel, the veteran ferryman, wrestled in the awning from his *Gertrude*. All, like the spider, sensed a blow and took their precautions.

The dense cloud to the west blackened further and squeezed toward the water.

Shortly a funnel reached down some distance off Sherod's Reef. A waterspout arched to the surface. Now a waterspout, while not an everyday affair, is relatively common along the south shore of Lake Erie, particularly around Vermilion. Here the land-heated wind blowing from the west suddenly finds itself over a cooler body of water due to the shape of the shoreline. The lower temperature reduces the volume of the air and thus lowers the cloud. One wild afternoon, my father, the old Commodore, and I watched some eight waterspouts carry eastward and north of the lighthouse.

The waterspout which Burns and I were observing was due west of and coming directly toward the light. While no structure is immune to the power of tempest unleashed, those of you who recall the old lighthouse will remember it being extremely ruggedly built. Actually the octahedral walls were of cast-iron. These sections sat on and were bolted to each other forming a gently tapering and truncated octahedron crowned by the window lantern for the light.

Now waterspouts had never hit the light since its erection in 1877, for their course was always northeastward. Enamored by the sight, Burns and I stopped our cleaning, our eyes glued to the waterspout bearing toward us. Dark and towering it came, dusting the water surface, and smoking at its foot. Elemental nature is seldom mild. What a place to develop humility to the Lord.

Presently the wind stiffened and sliced off the wave tops to sing through the air. The waterspout grew and came due east. It was now at the water-intake-buoy. A swell danced at its foot. Coming slowly forward, the funnel serpentined and twisted. As this majestic shape strode on, it was apparent, if the waterspout were this time to miss the light the distance would be short.

We could see the counter-clock rotation of the funnel, thundering and accompanied by shattering lightning. The cloud-funnel above was physically mirrored in the water below. This phenomenon is not unlike the way in which water in a sink swirls and recesses in the center when the drain-plug is pulled. But here, multiplied a thousand-fold, was a maelstrom. The rapidly twisting lake water at the foot of the waterspout was depressed like a funnel, reaching to the lake bottom.

On came this Vision, writhing, threshing, and forking with lightning, like a dozen express trains in sound, but snail-like in pace. The lighthouse now shuddered as the blast struck. The hinge-bolts in the thick steel-plate door rattled. The lightning rod, pointing skyward from the roof, sliced the air and sung from vibration. The spinning cone, like a whirling dervish, neared the rock solid light, veered and passed less than a dozen feet from the rocks at the pier end. At the center of the vortex, the lake bottom was clearly seen.

At this instant a bolt of purple lightning descended the towering and whirling shaft into the vortex. A flash of fire burst forth and a unique green light struck my left eye from the Fresnel prism surrounding the light. A unique green hue entered my subconscious mind. A hue I would long remember.

A VISION OF GOLD

The storm passed and the years rolled away. The light was made automatic. I grew up and entered college. There, at the University of Michigan, I pursued a scientific field of study. I had one course in Light and Optics, given by the late Professor Charles F. Meyers, now long dead. In that course I studied identification of elements by their characteristic spectra.

For these experiment I had an arc source of electricity and a series of elements such as copper, lead, tin, iron, aluminum, mercury, gold, and carbon. Each of these elements in turn I would mount on the electrode, apply the electricity, and an arc would form. The light emitted from the arc, when observed through a prism, would be characteristic of the element on the electrode, just as a finger print is characteristic of a particular person and of no one else.

I would direct the emitted light through a prism in order to better separate the character of the light, similarly as one, in studying a fingerprint, would use a magnifying glass to better resolve the whorls of the finger.

Successively carrying on these experiment, I observed the spectrum of iron, of aluminum, of copper, of gold. Of gold, a unique green hue came from the prism, matching in color that light which, fifteen years earlier, had arisen from nature's lightning arcing on the lake bottom. And that element was gold! There again was the prism, the lens in the lighthouse. Now the prism was part of a laboratory experiment.

Resting back in my chair at the laboratory, I dreamed back more than a dozen years and realized that some dozen feet off and northwestward from the pier-end was a cache of gold, pure, yellow, and noble. Possibly the sack binding the ingots was now water-rotted and surely charred from the lightning which I had so singularly observed. The heavy gold would long remain unyielding and resolute.

Why, you may ask, have I not sought this hoard of yellow metal?

Well, you earlier Vermilion residents may remember that the old light started leaning crazily into the river. My father called the U. S. Corp of Engineers. In their subsequent observation they removed the 1877 Vermilion Lighthouse then rebuilt and extended the pier-end. The old light was replaced with the frugal steep-sided, truncated pyramid which now serves nightly, to identify Vermilion harbor. This reconstruction was done in 1929. I went to college in 1933, so neither the U.S. Engineers nor myself, at that time, realized the new foundation of the light covered sacks of gold. Only I have realized it since. It is in this book, at long last, I pass this secret on to you.

Burns and I were washing the lantern windows.
Photojournal: Wally Wheatley

The 1877 lighthouse was replaced by a pyramidal light in 1929. George P. Wakefield.

APPENDIX F

(actual copy received by Theodore D. Wakefield from U. S. Lighthouse Service: Editor)

Vermilion light-station, Ohio
Lake Erie.

(Established in 1847. Rebuilt in 1859, & 1877.

Appropriated by act of Congress, for a beacon-light, & preparing the head of the pier for the same, at Vermilion River, Ohio,	- Mar. 3, 1847,	$3000.
" For renewing the light at Vermillion harbor, & repairing the pier on which it is placed,	Aug.31, 1852,	3000.
" For repaing the lt-ho. pier at Vermilion,	- March 3, 1859,	5000.
" For a dwelling for the keeper of Vermilion lt-ho.,	- Mar. 3, 1871,	4000.

1859 Vermillion pier and beacon and Coneaut light-house have been rebuilt.

1868 33. *Vermillion beacon.*—The tower, a small structure of wood, has been forced out of perpendicular by the action of the waves in gales of wind and requires repair.

1869 40. *Vermillion Beacon.*—The wooden tower, the only structure on this station, is in good condition. There is no dwelling for the keeper at this station.

1870 425. *Vermillion, Ohio, Lake Erie.*—This light station has not been provided with a dwelling for the light keeper. An appropriation is asked, of $4,000, for the purchase of a site, to erect a suitable frame dwelling and for repairs of the pier of protection to the light.

1871 483. *Vermillion,* Ohio, Lake Erie.—An appropriation was made March 3, 1871, for building a light-keeper's dwelling at this station. The station was visited May 18 for the purpose of selecting and purchasing a suitable site. No suitable vacant lot could be purchased that was easily accessible from the piers, and from which the beacon could be seen, and in consequence a purchase was made of a lot with a new house upon it, containing every convenience for a keeper's dwelling. Occupation will take place when the papers necessary for vesting title in the United States have been examined and approved by the Attorney General.

1872 499. *Vermillion, Lake Erie, Ohio.*—The house and lot purchased in this village for the use of the light-keeper were transferred to the United States in April. A few alterations have been made to the house to furnish accommodations for oil, and a cellar, a neat inclosure, and a stone sidewalk have been added. The station is in fine order.

1877

555. *Vermillion, Vermillion Harbor, Lake Erie, Ohio.*—The tower is old, decayed, and in danger of falling down. A new iron tower has been ordered to replace it. The elevated walk will also be extended to the shore.

1878

556. *Vermillion, Lake Erie, Ohio.*—The old beacon-tower has been pulled down and replaced by a new one of iron, resting upon an oak foundation forming the top of the old crib, and supporting a new lantern of the sixth order. The old sixth-order light has been replaced by one of the fifth order.

1880

590. *Vermillion, entrance to Vermillion Harbor, Lake Erie, Ohio.*—The elevated walk was rebuilt for a distance of 620 feet. At the opening of navigation the color of the light was changed to red. The beacon was repainted and some slight repairs were made.

an. R 1887.

827. *Vermillion, entrance to Vermillion Harbor, Lake Erie, Ohio.*—The upper timber course of the foundation supporting the iron tower was renewed and leveled, and minor repairs were made.

1892

1052. *Vermillion, on the outer end of the west pier, entrance to Vermillion Harbor, Lake Erie, Ohio.*—The base of the beacon was protected with plank sheathing to prevent the direct action of the water upon the bed timbers during high winds, which had been hastening their decay. The elevated walk leading to the tower and the plank walk about the keeper's dwelling were repaired with new material, and the stone sidewalk around the light-house reservation was raised and leveled to conform to the adjoining walks.

1893

1079. *Vermillion, on the outer end of the west pier, entrance to Vermillion Harbor, Lake Erie, Ohio.*—On April 27, 1893, the light-tower on the west pier was struck by the schooner *M. S. Bacon*, while she was being towed out of the harbor by the steam tug *J. P. Devney*. Two angle-iron plates in the second section of the tower were so badly injured that new plates had to be made to replace them. Many of the joints between the outer plates of the tower were strained, the interior somewhat injured, and one corner of the beacon raised about 2 inches. The beacon was repaired and a bill for the cost was presented to the owners of the *Devney*. They declined to pay it. The case was turned over to the Department of Justice, that proper legal proceedings might be taken.

1894

1101. *Vermillion, entrance to Vermillion Harbor, Lake Erie, Ohio.*—The iron beacon was moved to within about 25 feet of the outer end of the pier and the timbers of the beacon foundation, which were decayed, were replaced. Some 56 running feet of elevated walk was built to connect the beacon in its new position with the old walk. In April, 1893, the schooner *M. S. Bacon*, in tow of the tug *J. P. Devney*, collided with the beacon in such a manner as to cause serious injury. Repairs were made and the expense, $161.62, was collected and paid into the U. S. Treasury by the U. S. attorney at Cleveland, Ohio. Various minor repairs were made.

1897

1233. *Vermillion, entrance to Vermillion Harbor, Lake Erie, Ohio.*—About 100 feet of elevated walk on the west pier was rebuilt. Various repairs were made.

1898

1255. *Vermillion, entrance to Vermillion Harbor, Lake Erie, Ohio.*—Some 360 feet of elevated walk on the west pier was repaired.

1901 *105. Vermilion, entrance to Vermilion Harbor, Lake Erie, Ohio.*— About 186 feet of elevated walk on the west pier was rebuilt. Minor repairs were made to the keeper's dwelling.

1904 *107. Vermilion, entrance to Vermilion Harbor, Lake Erie; Ohio.*— About 120 running feet of elevated walk was rebuilt. Various repairs were made.

1905 *107. Vermilion, entrance to Vermilion Harbor, Lake Erie, Ohio.*— The materials for 500 running feet of iron walk to be erected on the west pier were purchased; also the metal work for an iron oilhouse. Various repairs were made.

1906 *106. Vermilion, entrance to Vermilion Harbor, Lake Erie, Ohio.*— An iron oilhouse, with a capacity of 540 gallons, was built. About 500 running feet of iron elevated walk was built on the west pier and about 63 running feet of wooden walk was rebuilt.

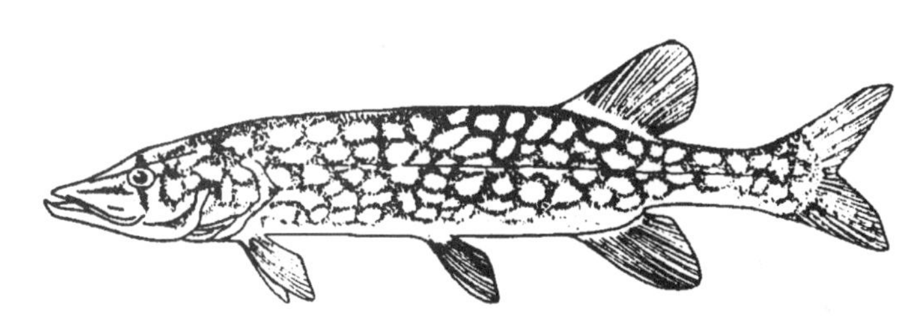

Chain pickerel. *Basics of Fishing*

APPENDIX G

ARCHITECTURAL NOTES AND ERECTION of the REPLICA VERMILION LIGHTHOUSE

Randy K. Strauss

Below is the diary of Randy K. Strauss, co-director of the Management Team along with Robert Lee Tracht, architect, for design, overseeing construction, site preparation, placement and erection of the replica Vermilion lighthouse. Posterity is fortunate in having these notes. They would not exist except for the thoroughness of Strauss and the alertness of Theodore D. Wakefield of the Steering Committee. Like records may never have been written for the construction and placement of the 1877 Vermilion lighthouse. In what follows RKS represents Strauss. Editor.

Wednesday 9/25/91 (Clear 58°F. @ 7:33 a.m., pred. good weather)

-11:00 a.m. Randy & Jim Lichtenberg met with Dave Phillips of Valley Harbor Marina at the the Museum. Jim and RKS laid out the elevations and rough dig area.

-Dave Phillips with his backhoe, dug out the existing hill and flattened the site for foundation excavation.

-Dave finished the site excavation at 2:30 -+p.m.

Thursday 9/26/91 (Partly cloudly 54°F @ 11:56 a.m., strong NW wind)

-Due to weather predictions of high winds, gale force winds and waves, sleet and rain —Randy, Dan Strauss & Jim Lichtenberg collectively decided to postpone all activities and reschedule for Monday. Also considered was the Woolly Bear Festival scheduled for this Sunday (in Vermilion) and the

Randy K. Strauss in center. M. R. Wakefield.

Lowering the lantern. M. R. Wakefield.

number of persons that might be exposed to the problem.

-RKS installed caution tape around excavation.

Friday 9/27/91 (Clear, clouds on lake, 44°F @ 7:46a.m., pred. sun, clouds, rain - a mess?)

-No work was done today, excavation is scheduled for Monday.

Sat. - No work.

Sunday - Woolly Bear Sunday - no work.

Monday 9/30/91 (Clear & sunny, 54° F @ 7:58 a.m. pred. Rain, fair, & cool)

-Randy called excavator - we are scheduled to start layout and exca vation at 11:00 today.

-RKS leaving for Columbus – Jim will supervise today.

-J.L. reported (Gillen Excavating)

-He arrived 11:15 a.m., Dave & Wilby were already on site (Dave Mullen & Jim Welburn).

-They excavated actual footings and found rubble and sand pockets in the front half (N. side) of the footing.

-They finished at approx. 3:30 p.m.

Tuesday 10/1/91 (Clear, 66°F @ 7:52 a.m., pred. P. cldy & warm)

-J.L. informed RKS of the footing bottom referred to above.

-RKS placed a call for Bob Tracht @ 7:45 a.m., and left a message on his answer(ing) machine.

-RKS talked to Bob T. - he'll go out and investigate foundation this afternoon.

-Bob called me this afternoon at approx. 3:30 p.m. - he said to pour a 12" min. thick spread footing, full width of dig - the form on top of the footing, less one foot as per plans. Use 3 #4 (1/2" dia.) steel rods in pour - no need for chains, just drop in pour.

Wednesday 10/2/91 (Clear, 72°F @ 9:54 a.m., pred. warm, pos. rain).

-RKS met w/ Steve H(ull) from Hull Concrete @ 7:00 a.m. @ light house site - concrete & steel ordered for this afternoon flat footer pour.

-RKS, Chris Battistelli (labored for Strauss), Gene Darby (a retired volunteer), Jim Lichtenberg and Pete Lorandeau (Vermilion Building Inspector – helped for a while), all set grade pins, set steel tack bars for the angle steel template and poured 8 yards of concrete for the foundation as instructed by the Architect Bob Tracht.

-Schedule is to build and set sidewall concrete forms Thurs. and set steel template and pour concrete on Friday.

Thursday 10/3/91 (Raining 64°F @ 8:00 a.m., pred. clear, then rain)

-Carpenter went home in a.m. due to rain.

-Rain cleared and sun came out in p.m.

-Carpenter gone - no forms built – we will not be able to pour the upper foundation tomorrow - rain is predicted for tomorrow anyhow.

Friday 10/4/91 (Rain, T. showers, heavy, 64°F @ 7:45 a.m., pred. rain)

-Carpenters were rained out yesterday so sidewall forms were built or set – rain this morning – RKS called all volunteers and cancelled today's work, will try again next week.

No work over weekend

Monday 10/7/91 (Sun mixed w/ Lake effect clouds, 56°F 3:47 p.m. Breezy @ cool)

-Duane Highland and three of his carpenters started to build the 8 forms for the 2nd foundation pour. Being built @ a remote location.

-We plan on picking up the forms tomorrow morning - delivery to the museum and erecting.

-If weather holds we will set steel and pour concrete on Wednesday.

-RKS called Joe Whelan of Roth Manufacturing @ 3:55 - will call later this week to arrange a meeting w/ crane operators.

Tuesday 10/8/91 (Sunny, 68°F @ 5:27 p.m., Beautiful, light S. wind)

-8:00 a.m. RKS (I) picked up the forms from a house site where they were built yesterday

-8:20 a.m. - RKS, Jim L., Duane Highland and three of his carpenters (Matt Brletic, Mark Pitcher & Richard Johnston) arrived at museum. Dan Strauss also helped.

-We set forms, getting a true square was real tough with the octagon shape.

-We braced the forms and set the steel anchor bolt patterns in place.

-Dave Phillips from Valley Harbor came over about 2:00 p.m. and welded everything in place.

-We are scheduled for 1:00 p.m. pour tomorrow.

Wednesday 10/9/91 (partly cloudy, 62°F @ 7:27 a.m., pred. showers).

-RKS, Jim L. & Gene Darby arrived at site at 9:30 a.m. - we set 1 1/2" PVC (EMT conduit) to act as vents and drains. Garth Grobe of Tri-Power Elec. supplied the PVC and some tools.

-Garth Grobe and one man (name?) arrived on site and ran the electricconduit through the foundation formwork and ran an electric outlet out of the museum.

-At 1:45 two men from Jim Gillen Concrete arrived with a truck full of tools and equipment (Rick Smith of North Ridgeville and Stacy Davis of Elyria)

-Hull Concrete sent (thanks to Steve Hollfax) 10 1/2 yards of concrete - we poured the base foundation and vibrated it. There was extreme pressure against the forms - we heard one loud crack, form oil was pushed through the O.S.B. sheating - we reinforced as well as possible and completed the pour.

-We finished the concrete & covered the pour with Visqueen.

Left the job at 5:50 p.m.

Thursday 10/10/91 (Raining, 56°F @ 8:40 a.m., showers - clearing)

RKS checked the site @ 6:40 a.m. - everything looked good - we will strip the forms tomorrow.

Friday 10/11/91 (Raining, 54°F @ 7:35 a.m., pred. cloudy & rain).

-RKS & Chris loaded up the truck and arrived @ lighthouse site @ 8:00 a.m.

-Dan Strauss & Gordon Welty also helped.

-We stripped all formwork, scraped all steel, ground all sharp edge concrete and cleaned up site - we finished @ 11:00 a.m. -took all scrap materials to the Vermilion Police picnic grounds (for Charlie Grisel's bonfire/clam bake).

-RKS saw John Herkler from Herk Excavating @ the site - I asked him if he could backfill and grade - he said OK.

-RKS called Jack Malloy of Malloy Masonry - I asked if he could Through-Seal the foundation on Sat., he said yes provided it is not raining.

Monday 10/14/91 (Overcoat, 48°F @ 9:20 a.m., showers predicted).

-Jack Malloy had applied Through-Seal to the exposed foundation either on Saturday or Sunday.

RKS set up an inspection of the fabricated lighthouse at Milan Fabricators with Joe Whelan (of Roth Manufacturing), Dick Decker (crane operator), Dan Strauss, Jim Litchenberg, & RKS.

Tuesday 10/15/91 (Partly sunny, 44°F @ 7:30 a.m., pred. cloudy & rain p.m.)

-RKS stopped at jobsite at 2:00 p.m.

-A crew from B.M.D. Dock & Dredge was at the site of the pilot house (of the museum), they were working on welding & setting the gang walks.

-I called for Bob Tracht - left message.

-Dick Decker called, we rescheduled tomorrow's meeting at Milan Fabricators for 3:30 p.m. tomorrow.

Wednesday 10/16/91 (Sunny, 48°F @ 9:24 a.m., clear but cool pred.)

-RKS, Jim L., Dan Strauss met Bob Tracht (architect), Dick Decker (crane operator/owner), Joe Whelan (Roth Manufacturing) and others at Milan Fabricators.

-The lower section of the lighthouse was approximately 80% complete, the top section (lantern) has not yet been started.

-We discussed (among other things) shipping/trucking, permits, crane hoisting, unloading & lifting, anchor bolts, rubber seals, clearances tolerances, etc.

-We are hoping for delivery on Tuesday October 22, 1991.

Thursday 10/17/91 (Sunny 60°F @ 3:00 p.m. -beautiful).

No activity today, except Joe Whelan called to say he still had no info on the hauling permit at that time. He'll call Friday.

Friday 10/18/91 (Sunny 63°F @ 11:20 a.m., cooling tonight).

-RKS saw John Herkler (Herk Excavating) and asked if he could back fill foundation - John said he thought he could do it this weekend.

-RKS spoke to Dick Decker -Dick said he needed to apply for his "oversized load" permit necessary to move the 35 ton crane - Dick also said he would provide the second, smaller crane that we'll need to unload the unit.

-Tom Barker of Roth Manufacturing called @ 12:50 p.m. and said permit was approved for a Wednesday (Oct. 23rd) move. The transport company is McGill Transport. We still don't know what time or if it can be delayed due to weather conditions.

Monday 10/21/91 (Sunny, 52°F @ 10:45 a.m., pred. warming & nice).

-John Herkler (Herk Excavating) knocked down hillside and rough graded foundation.

-8:15 a.m. Joe Whelan called - said to expect delivery at approx. 1:00 p.m. on Wednesday (10/23), I told him to try earlier as much was needed to be done that day. He said he'd try and would call me later today.

-Joe called back - lighthouse leaves @ 9:00 a.m. - allow approximately one-hour to site.

Tuesday 10/22/91 (Sunny, 55°F @ 9:00a.m., pred. warm & sunny).

-Dan Strauss cut screening and inserted it into 1 1/2" PVC drain & vent pipes, and cut off vent tops.

-Joe Whelan called - lighthouse top (lantern) may not be ready tomor row and may be delivered later - if so, Roth Mfg. will supply the crane to set it.

Wednesday 10/23/01 (Mostly sunny, 62°F @ 7:59 a.m., pred. warm & sunny).

-RKS arrived at the lighthouse site @ 9:30 a.m. Dick Decker (Crane Rental Services, Inc.) already had two cranes on site and set up. Apparently done last night.

-First chase vehicle arrived at 10:15 - had to go back to Milan, meet truck and then travel back to Vermilion - now expected time between noon & 12:30 p.m. (originally scheduled for delivery 10:00 - 10:30 a.m.

-Truck with lighthouse arrived on site at 12:15 - from unloading and standing lighthouse upright, to setting the lighthouse on its foundation took approximately 1 1/2 hours.

-The top portion (lantern) of the structure was not yet complete and would have to be sent on Thursday.

-RKS completed all work and left the site at approximately 3:30 p.m.

Thursday 10/24/91 (Sunny 80°F @ 1:45 p.m., pred. rain late).

-Dan Strauss called Joe Whelan of Roth Mfg. to see what time the top portion (lantern) of the lighthouse would be delivered - Joe expected 2:00 p.m. - they (Roth) would arrange for crane and welding at site.

-Dan Strauss went to site @ 2:00 p.m. - the people from Milan Fabricators (including Joe Whelan), with the top portion of the light house on a low-boy truck had been there since 12:00 noon. The crane arrived @ (about) 2:30 and set the unit on the lower base.

-Apparently some discussion transpired regarding the location of the upper door.

-RKS arrived on site @ 3:30 p.m. - Milan Fabricators people were welding the unit into place, making adjustments, etc.

Friday 10/25/91 (Light rain, 69°F @ 8:00 a.m., T. storm pred. warm).

Monday 10/28/91 (Overcast, 54°F @ 7:50 a.m., strong N. winds, predicted cloudy & cool).

-RKS did not visit site.

Tuesday10/29/91 (Sunny a.m., 60°F @ 4:30 p.m., turned cloudy, cool & drizzle).

-Talked to Fox Painting of Fremont - he estimated prime & finish paint @ $2,600.00.

Thursday 10/31/91 (Overcast 55°F @ 3:45 p.m., low/no wind -no rain).

-RKS did not visit site.

Friday 11/1/91 (Sunny a.m., turned overcast, 68°F @ 4:35 p.m/. rain tonight).

-RKS did not visit site.

Monday 11/4/91 (Sunny, 23°F @ 8:40 a.m., cold w/snow possible).

-RKS talked with Bob Tracht - he said he sent Fox Painting bid on to museum officials - (the) bid was $2,600 complete.

-Bob also said that he had received a verbal bid from Northern Ohio Roofing, but still had not received the written proposal.

-RKS did mention to Bob that the upper door (going outside to the cat walk) was hinged wrong with hinges on the South side, Bob was going to check on this.

Tuesday 11/5//91 (Sunny 14°F @ 7:40 a.m., record cold, pred. 30's)

-No further work has been done since the day the lighthouse was set & top cap put on.

Wednesday 11/6/91 (Overcast 41°F @ 8:30 a.m., pred. snow)

-RKS did not visit site.

Thursday 11/7/91 (Snowy 32°F - snowed most of day).

-RKS did not visit site.

Friday 11/8/91 (Sunny 30°F @ 8:10 a.m., Ptly cloudy & cold tonight).

-I hope that Roth Mfg. did not put/leave the paint inside the lighthouse as I'm sure it will now be frozen.

Monday 11/11/91 (Overcast, 43°F @ 9:40 a.m., pred. rain then clear'g).

-RKS stopped by, no more work has been done since we stood the unit up.

Tuesday 11/12/91 (Overcast 38°F @ 9:00 a.m., pred. rain).

-RKS did not visit site today.

Wednesday11/13/91 (Overcast 47°F @ 2:30 p.m., pred. clearing).

-Dick Decker called and said he wanted to send a bill for donating purposes - approximate cost about $2,400 - I told him to send to me addressed Great Lakes Historical Society.

Thursday 11/14/91 RKS out of town, business.

Friday 11/15/91 RKS out of town business.

Monday 11/18/91 RKS did not visit site.

Tuesday 11/19/91 RKS did not visit site.

-Garth Grobe called asking about completion, I gave him the architect's phone number. Garth mentioned the possibility of putting an outlet in the the base where his conduit enters and running a simple chord to the light at the top - I again referred him to the architect on the job.

Wednesday 11/20/91 (Overcast, light rain 69°F @ 7:50 a.m., pred. rain).

Thursday 11/21/91 (Overcast, rain 48°F @ 5:06 p.m., -rain pred.).

-RKS did not visit site.

END

Vermilion river looking north through the piers to Lake Erie. On the left moored the lighthouse tender *Haze* in 1877, the *La Belle* in 1911, the Coast Guard cutter *CG-219* in 1927, the derrick barge *Erie* in 1929, and daily the steam fishing tugs passed.
Theodore D. Wakefield.

APPENDIX H

CONTRIBUTORS TO THE REPLICA LIGHTHOUSE

As collated by Martha Long of the Inland Seas Maritime Museum

The planning, building, erecting, and fund raising of the 1877 Vermilion Lighthouse replica was a community enterprise executed under the guidance of :

Steering Committee

William T. Stark
John Trinter
Theodore D. Wakefield

Management Team

Robert Lee Tracht, Architect
Randy Strauss, Foundation and Erection

Fabricator

Roth Manufacturing Corporation

Gifts in Kind

Mr. & Mrs. Theodore D. Wakefield II
Vermilion Jaycees
The Cargo Warehouse
Vermilion Photojournal
USS/Kobe Steel Co.
Roth Commercial
Otto Kirchner
Edmund J. O'Brien
Robert Doane
Tri-Power Electric Co.
Fraser Shipyards, Inc.
The Harbour Store 1847
Hull Concrete Co.
Lakeland Glass Co.
Nautical Notions

Companies Donating Services

Decker Crane Service,Inc.
Herk Excavating Co.
Gillen Concrete Co.
Jack Malloy's Masonry
Gillen Excavating Co.
Strauss Construction Co.
Duane Heiland, General Contractor
Valley Harbor Marina

Individuals Donating Labor and Time

Matt Brletic
Jack Malloy
Gene Darby
David Mullen
Stacy Davis
David Phillips
Dick Decker
Mark Pitcher

H2

Duane Heiland Rick Smith JohnHerchler Pete Lorandeau

Richard Johnston Dan Strauss Jim Welburn Gordon Welty

Jim Lichtenberg

Donor	In Honor Of
Robert H. Bailey	Henry G. Bailey
Fred Bark	Bark Auction and Realty
Daniel Beifuss	Beverly Beifuss
Don and Diane Chesnut	Henry G. Bailey
Stephen W. Cole	The Cole Family
James Fischer Family	Mari-Dor Beach
Marilyn J. Gallandt	Great Lake Lighthouse Keepers' Association
Xin Bao Gino	Vermilion Lighthouse
Bill & Karen O'Malley	Carolyn & Chuck Dewey
John B. & Deborah D. Pecorak	T. D. Wakefield & his grandchildren, John, Katherine, & Sara
Claude Rahl	Ganbe Brown
Boyd & Mary Jo Robinson	Dean Runkle
Larry & Joan Rolince	Larry & Joan Rolince
Mr.& Mrs. John B. Sadler	Elizabeth K. Sadler
A. E. Szambecki	The Szambecki Family
Vermilion Hardware Co.	Henry G. Bailey
Mare & Gregory C. Wakefield	Bernadette Parsons Wakefield
Margaret A. Wakefield	Theodore D. Wakefield
Theodore D. Wakefield	Margaret R. Read, M.D.
Danny N. & Diana L. Young	Lois E. Smith Blanchard

Donor	In Memory Of
Lee Patterson Allen	Clara & Hyatt M. Patterson
	Fred and Lee Patterson

H3

Margaret Bracco	Clara Wakefield Hofrichter
Elaine Brady	Jerome Brady
Jeane Marie Burns	Anna Zielkowski
Nancy Stutz Butler	Ruth Wakefield Stutz
Mary Wakefield Buxton	Aunt Lydie Wakefield
Jan, Dianna & Mary Clark	Capts. Charles & James Gegenheimer
Lois & Susan Diesing	Arthur Van Dyke
Dr. & Mrs William Ferber	Ella A. Campbell
Mrs. Robert Filker	Robert Filker
Mr. & Mrs. Ronald Coleman & Family	
Mr. & Mrs. Richard Smith & Family	
Mr. & Mrs. Paul Coleman & Family	
Mr. & Mrs. Donald Manly & Family	
Alan & Karen Ganim	Fred & Mary Jane Kubishke
Lucile E. Hite	Arthur Hite
Diane Howell	William J. Wakefield
Robert & Carol Jones	George R. Jones
Forest A. Judy	Capt. George Reiber
Lester H. Kishman	H. B. Kishman
Richard H. Knell	Riechmann P. Knell
Mrs. Reichmann P. Knell & Family	Riechmann P. Knell
	George (Pete) Wahl Family
	Annetta Wahl Otto Family
Adele Kovanic	John & Elizabeth Kovanic
Margaret B. Krantz	William J. Krantz
Lillian Steane Lewis	Emily Wakefield Copeland
	Wm. A. & Sarah Copeland Steane
Mr. & Mrs. David H. McFarland	Mr. & Mrs. Arthur O'Hara

Mr. & Mrs Jack McGahey	Alfred Weber
Adrienne Mather	Judy Mather
Mr. & Mrs. Charles F. Milner, Jr.	Frederick Wright Wakefield
Arlene Minch	Ray & Sharon Minch
Shirley M. Molnar	Barbara M. Gendics
William Morehouse Family	Pennie Morehouse
Jean & Pat Owen	Capt. George W. Reiber
Christine & Matthew Owen	
Harold J. Rathbun	Captain George S. Rathbun
Phyllis M. Read	Loretta M. Read
Carlton & Anna Laura Richie	Dr. Emil J. Heinig & Family
Jim & Patti Ryder	Mrs. Avis L. Owen
Dave & Pat Scharra	Irvin Scharra
Thomas & Barbara Smigelski	Ted Smigelski
Mr. & Mrs. Terry L. Smith	Raymond M."Gunner" Smith
Marie & Charles Tansey	Art & Muriel O'Hara
Donald C. Trinter	Elmer & Ruth Trinter
Ann Mary Wakefield	Hilda Gertrude Wakefield
Bernadette P. Wakefield	Fred W. Wakefield
Ernest Henry Wakefield	Frederick William Wakefield
George P. Wakefield	John G. Robinson,1883-1984
Mare & Gregory C. Wakefield	Frederick Wright Wakefield, Sr.
Margaret Read Wakefield	Loretta M. & Fred K. Read, M.D.
Mary B. Wakefield	Alice Parsons Baldridge, 1888-1938
Danny N. & Diana L. Young	Harold E. Smith

Donors

AARP, Vermilion Chapter	Amvets Auxiliary
Ade Skunta Company	Richard A. Anjesky

H5

Henry G. Bailey
Peter & Graham Bateman
Scott Bauman
Betty & Jack Bechtel
Peggy Bechtol
Ercil Beck
Daniel Bennett
Brummer's
Dr. & Mrs. James D. Burson
Jay & Joyce Carson
Jay & Joyce Carson
Centel Corporation
Chamber of Commerce
Mr. & Mrs. M.R. Cicerchi
Solomon Cohen
Clayton M. Cook
Harold C. Copperman, D.D.S.
John & Cindy Costin
Willis Darby
Al & Sandi Davis
Darryl & Mary Ann Dobras
Don's Guns & Ammo
Marion Wakefield Stutz Droege
Constance S. Dropko
Charles L. Duggan
George J. & Becky Dunn
EST Bank
F. H. Ellenburger

Paul Farace
James Fasnacht
Kenneth C.Fitchel
Friends of Harbor Town
Mr. & Mrs. Robert Fritz
Fred & Jill Fryberger
Thomas W. Furey
Charles & Pamela Fury
Mark & Carolyn Gagyi
Ron & Barb Gerken
Sandi Gerstacker
Albert D. Gilchrist
Gimben Gallery
Linda Glade
Nancy Godley
Marian Greene
Evalene L. Greenwood
Pat Grego
Mr. & Mrs. David Groh
James C. Hageman
The Harbour Store 1847
Mr. & Mrs. David L. Herzer
Evelyn Hollis
Robert & Gloria Holtwick
Jack & Mary Hook
John L. Horton
Bill Immler
Alyce M. Jaeger

Mr. & Mrs James R. Jackson
H. R. Jameson
Jack R. & Janice R. Justice
Joseph M. Kaleel
Ross & Mary Anne Kingsley
Mr. & Mrs. Roy A. Kneisel
J. D. Lane
John Laslo
Mr. & Mrs. Charles Latto
Don & Kathy LeBeau
Frances G. Leidheiser
Paul & Catherine Leimkuehler
Lillian Steane Lewis
Martha Long
Mary Longbrake
Lorain National Bank
Walter & Bernadette McAllister
Mr. & Mrs James McClimans
Mr & Mrs. Edward McClurkin
Kenneth & Jerri McDaniel, Jr.
Gerald McFarland
Cury McGhee
James McKeen
Maple Grove Marina
Mr. & Mrs. Wiliam E. Market
Elizabeth Mason
Mrs. & Mrs. Jerry Massanova
Mr. & Mrs. Al Mastics

Mr. & Mrs. R. E. Maurer
Elmer R. & Audrey Meyers
Joe & Ann Miskow
Grant L. & Margaret H. Moyer
D. A. Nash
Karl & Sharon Newkirk
Melvin Niggle
Dennis & Joanne Norman
Mr. & Mrs. Clifford Oravec
Clarence & Helen Parsh
Mrs. Carolyn Perrusio
Capt. Grant Pettrie
Robert & Ellen Pierce
Patricia E. Pine
William H. Posegate
Jack Power
David L. & Elfriede K. Prusa
Lou & Dorothy Rauh
Shirley Reeve
John L. Reulbach
Ben Richmond
Larry & Joan Rolince
Robert & Helen C. Root
Brad R. Schwab
Richard A. Sirocky
Evelyn E. Smith
Laura Jean Smith
Mr. & Mrs. Fred L. Snow

Robert P. Sperling
W. Thomas & Faye L. Stahl
William T. Stark
William G. Wickens
Andrew Sterling
Rita Howley Summers
Philip G. Tarr
William D. (Bud) Taylor
Sean Templeton
Earl Tischer
June Travis
John D. Tregembo, Sr.
Elizabeth Trinter
Lawrence R. Uebbing
Stephen Ulasik
Ernest Vagi
Mr. & Mrs. Ronald A. Van Den Bossche
Robert W. Van Hengel
Oscar Van Loveren
Dr. & Mrs. Paul F. Varley
Vermilion Foundation Fund
Robert & Marjorie Via
Paul Von Gunten
Dr. & Mrs. John F. Wakefield
Read, Lynda & Amy Wakefield, Alison & Sara Marconi
Mr. & Mrs. Theodore D. Wakefield
Theodore D. Wakefield II
Roger & Sue Watkins
Grant & Marian Winterfield
Charles L. Worchester
Alma Zager
Dr. & Mrs. Thomas F. Zeck
Anonymous (13)

Addendum

Vermilion Harbor Yacht Club
Society Bank
Ann J. Oestermeyer

Dear Pres. Bush,

Please put the lighthouse back in Vermilion, Ohio.

Sean Templeton (8 years of age - Huron, Ohio).

GLOSSARY

Carline: a rafter which supports the roof.

Echelon: an apparatus of high dispersive and resolving power, consisting of a series of plane parallel glass plates so arranged that the edges, each overlapping its neighbor by the same amount, resemble a flight of stairs. The plates are of equal thickness. See illustration of the Fresnel lens in the body of the text.

Fender streak: a structure designed to be protective of the main body, be it the hull of a vessel or the base of a lighthouse.

Fresnel lens: a form of echelon lens designed especially for use in lighthouses. By its use the light from a luminous source is emitted in a parallel beam. Named after its inventor the French physicist Augustin Jean Fresnel,1788-1827.

Gaff hook: an iron hook with a handle suitable for securing a heavy fish.

Gill net: a mesh standing as a fence across the bottom of a body of water. Floats support the upper edge, sinkers anchor the lower. A fish striking the net is caught by its gills.

Gillnetter: a vessel which catch fish by means of gill nets.

Gland or stuffing box: a device to prevent leakage along the rudderpost to the rudder. It consists of a box made by enlarging the hole, and a gland or follower to compress the contained packing.

Lantern: that section of a lighthouse which encloses the light source.

Lightning rod: an invention of Benjamin Franklin, American philosopher and statesman, 1706-1790. Franklin flew a kite in a rainstorm. To the ground end of the string he tied a key. Sparks were observed to jump from key to any nearby object. (A Russian repeating this experiment in St. Petersburg was killed). Franklin found these sparks would ignite a watch glass of alcohol. Earlier he observed a glass rod when rubbed with cat's fur would also emit sparks and ignite alcohol. Thus he correlated electricity found in lightning was the same as achieved from friction. Making this observation practical he reasoned a land-base structure such as a building or a lighthouse would be more immune from lightning if its topmost element was pointed so electrical charges would more easily leak into the atmosphere. This reduction of electrical potential-difference between cloud and object reduces the chance for a lightning strike.

Net: a fabric of twine woven into mesh and used to catch fish, insects, birds, and animals.

Order of a Fresnel lens: Captain R. A. Schultz of the Ninth U. S. Coast Guard District writes: "The term "order" as related to classical or Fresnel lenses refers to a classification of physical size. There are seven orders and each has a specific focal length and lens height as follows:

ORDERS	FOCAL LENGTHS (cm)	LENS HEIGHT (cm)
1	92	235
2	70	182
3	50	140
3 1/2	37.5	110
4	25	68
5	18.75	51
6	15	41

For a given light source the larger the lens, the brighter the light output. Modern lenses (express)...focal diameter in millimeters."

Pound net: a net to entrap fish. It consists of a long wing of net directing fishes into the heart and on through a check valve into an inner enclosure which has a closed bottom of net. The vertices are supported by posts. The latter section may be raised and the fish transferred to the fish boat.

Quadrant: a quarter circle, usually of metal, whose vertex is secured to the rudderpost. Cables connected to the ends of the quadrant's arc lead to a pulley on the steering wheel such that turning of the wheel steers the vessel.

Rib: a transverse member of the frame of a vessel, running from keel to deck and carrying the planking or plating of the hull.

Rudder post: a vertical shaft penetrating a vessel's hull, through a gland or stuffing box, to which the rudder is attached.

Stuffing box: see *gland* above.

Trapnetter: a fishing boat used to set trap nets in a body of water.

Whisker pole: a light wooden spar used to further spread a sail to catch more wind. In Admiral David Glascoe Farragut's order of the day preparatory to leading his fleet past Confederate-held Fort Morgan and into the Battle of Mobile Bay he wrote: "Strip your vessel and prepare for conflict. Send down all your superfluous spars and rigging. Trice up or remove the *whiskers.* Put up the splinter-nets on the starboard side, and barricade the wheel and steersmen with sails and hammocks...." The Battle of Mobile Bay (*"Damn the torpedoes, full speed ahead"*) was the largest sea battle fought by the U. S. Navy until the Spanish-American War of 1898.

INDEX

O

P

Q

R

S

NOTES

NOTES

NOTES

NOTES

NOTES

NOTES

NOTES

NOTES

NOTES

NOTES

NOTES

latter company he began designing electric cars. He conceived and his group delivered to Illinois Bell in 1968 the first alternating-current powered electric car ever sold anywhere. All automobile companies world-wide are now gearing up to make electric cars employing this principle.

He now devotes his time to writing having written *The Mystery of Fisherman's Reef* 1953, *Nuclear Reactors for Universities and Industries* 1957, *The Consumer's Electric Car* 1977, *Wakefield's History of the Electric Automobile: Battery-only Powered Electric Cars, International,* 1992, on solar-powered automobiles, and many papers on Third World economies. He has also written on the Medal of Honor, the 1863 U. S. Navy in the Pacific, nuclear fallout, and a three-volume love story *All Ages Succumb to Love.* Recently he edited *Wakefield's American Civil War Series, The Battle of Mobile Bay* 1990.

ABOUT THE AUTHOR

Ernest Henry Wakefield, author of *The Lighthouse That Wanted To Stay Lit*, was born on the second floor of the present Inland Seas Maritime Museum when the structure was the home of his family. He need only look north from his window to see the 1877 Vermilion Lighthouse, so naturally he has the fondest thoughts of this now long gone structure.

In the Preface Dr. Wakefield recounts the lighthouse was in his play area as a boy and coming from a yachting family he early welcomed its warm, red light. His earliest memory is from the berth of his father's yacht looking out the companionway onto the blue sky, and noticing the roll of the boat. His maritime interests result from owning eight boats from punts to an auxiliary ketch and three iceboats before he matriculated in college. For all the 1877 Vermilion Lighthouse was a rendezvous, summer and winter.

As a seventeen-old Wakefield sailed in the U. S. Merchant Marine steamship *Helen* of Wilmington, Delaware from whose decks he again became familiar with lighthouses and light-buoys.

Subsequently he would attend the University of Michigan and there earn a B.A. and a M.S. in Fine Arts, then later a Ph.D. in Electrical Engineering. On graduation Wakefield was employed in the Photometric Laboratory of the General Electric Company, subsequently the Westinghouse Corporation, and finally began teaching electrical engineering at the University of Tennessee in Knoxville. In World War II he volunteered into the Scientific Brigade of the Signal Corps of the U. S. Army. He was first ordered to the University of Chicago for further course work, then to the Massachusetts Institute of Technology where he participated in the RADAR program. Completing Basic Training Wakefield was then ordered to the University of Chicago and assigned to the Physics Division of the Manhattan Project, later popularly known as the Atom Bomb Project.

On discharge from the army he initiated a nuclear instrument company which became known world wide. Selling this organization, he established an import business employing many person in the Philippines and in Haiti. While operating the

(Continued on previous page)